# Too Soon to Say Good-bye

## Deborah Kent

AN
**APPLE**
PAPERBACK

SCHOLASTIC INC.
New York Toronto London Auckland Sydney

I would like to thank the nurses and doctors at St. Louis Children's Hospital who patiently answered my questions and searched out the odd tidbits of information I needed. I wish to express my special appreciation to Shawn Mayo for reviewing this manuscript, and for freely sharing with me the story of her own battle with leukemia.

ISBN 0-590-47798-6

12 11 10 9 8 7 6 5 4 3 2 1        6 7 8 9/9 0 1/0

Printed in the U.S.A.      40

First Scholastic printing, April 1996

# 1

My mother must have been psychic. The second I put down the dishrag she materialized in the kitchen doorway. "Did you wipe the counters?" she asked accusingly.

"Everything's done," I told her. "Just look around."

"What about that pot on the stove? It doesn't look done to me."

"Why can't Crysti do that one?" I protested. "She doesn't do anything around here!" I impatiently stamped my bare foot on the doormat. Amanda was waiting for me. I'd promised I'd be over right after supper.

Mom picked up the pot and tossed it into the sink. "I don't know what your hurry is," she remarked. "You and Amanda see each other practically twenty-four hours a day."

"I haven't seen her since yesterday morning! She had to go to her aunt's."

Mom reached for a Brillo pad. "Well," she said,

"you'd better run. You'd hate to miss out on the latest bulletin."

I opened the door and glanced back into the kitchen. Mom was up to her elbows in the dishwater, scrubbing the big pot she'd used for boiling the potatoes. She hadn't even called Crysti to come and help.

That was the way things worked in my family. Nobody ever expected Crysti to do many chores, or keep track of her library books, or pack her own lunch for school. She was only ten, after all. I was thirteen, my parents reminded me. If I wanted the privileges of being a teenager, I had to take a few responsibilities, too. The trouble was, my only privilege seemed to be a double helping of work around the house.

The instant I stepped outside, I forgot about the unfairness of it all. The August heat dropped over me like a fur coat, heavy and stifling. The air was so thick and steamy I could hardly get my breath, and the asphalt sidewalk scorched the soles of my bare feet. With a yelp of pain I hopped onto the grass, but that wasn't much better. By the time I was halfway across the yard I wanted to stagger back to the kitchen.

I should have invited Amanda to my house. But then Crysti would start snooping around, listening outside the door. On a cool day we could sneak away from her, through my closet, up the stairs, and into the attic. Our house was built in 1853,

2

and the attic was one of its special, secret places.

On a day like this, though, the attic would be an oven. No, I'd made the right decision. Getting out of my house was worth a bit of suffering.

At the end of our yard I stopped to rest at the Marlewskis' chain-link fence. The heat was so fierce I was starting to feel dizzy, but I knew I'd be all right once I got inside again. I shakily hoisted myself up and over the fence. Mr. Marlewski was really nice. He never complained that Amanda and I used his yard as our official shortcut, though sometimes he kidded us that he was going to set up a tollbooth.

Amanda's house shimmered before me like a desert mirage. I forced myself forward, step by step, but it didn't seem to come any closer.

"Jill! Wait up!"

Crysti's voice pulled at me from behind. I hadn't escaped after all. She was always trailing after me whenever I wanted to go anywhere alone.

"What are *you* doing here?" I demanded. "You should be helping Mom."

"She said it was okay," Crysti insisted, bearing down on me. "I want to come with you."

"Amanda's *my* friend!" I exclaimed. "Why don't you go play with Linda Sue?"

"She's still at camp," Crysti reminded me. "I haven't had anybody to hang around with all week! I'm dying of boredom."

The heat coiled around me, choking off my arguments. I thought of heading back home and trying to get Mom on my side, but I didn't have the energy. Besides, Mom would probably just tell me to be sisterly, so what was the use? "Okay," I said, shrugging my shoulders. "I'd hate to cause your untimely death or anything."

Crysti's eyes opened wide, and she gave a little skip of happiness. She hadn't expected me to cave in so easily. For a moment I felt like a princess, dispensing royal favors.

"Just don't be a pest," I added, to let her know I was in charge.

"Who, me?" she said, grinning. "A charming, beautiful, talented, creative, brilliant kid like me?"

"At least you didn't say *modest*," I said, clambering onto Amanda's porch at last. I stood in the tiny oasis of shade under the awning and knocked on the back door. The dog barked, but nobody came. My legs folded under me, and I sank onto the top step to wait. The maple tree in the yard seemed to be swaying strangely. But maybe I was the one who was teetering, tilting off balance.

"What's the matter?" Crysti demanded, leaning over to study my face. "You're a funny color."

"Gee, thanks," I said. My voice sounded far away.

"No, really," Crysti said. "You look kind of pasty."

"It's the heat. I can't stand it." I bent my head

down between my knees, and slowly my mind began to clear.

Behind me the door burst open. "Hey!" Amanda called. "Come on in before you melt."

"Hi," I said, getting to my feet. Amanda glanced at Crysti and shot me a questioning frown. "She swears she won't be a pest," I explained, and Crysti drew a cross in the air over her heart.

Amanda didn't complain. She was an only child, and she didn't usually mind when Crysti tagged along with us. I had to admit that I didn't really mind either, now that she was here. It wasn't that she did anything really awful. It was just the principle, the thought that I had to take her with me instead of having my best friend all to myself.

"You look like you just ran a marathon," Amanda commented, laughing. "It's not *that* bad out, is it?"

"I'm okay." *Pasty.* The word echoed inside my head. It sounded hideous. I wished I could cover my face with my hands, so no one could see the funny color I had turned.

Amanda didn't seem to notice, or else she was too polite to mention it. "Come have something cold," she said, and we trooped after her into the kitchen. I still felt a little light-headed when I sat at the table, in spite of the big ceiling fan that swept in slow circles overhead.

Amanda rattled ice cubes into glasses and

pulled a bottle of Sprite out of the fridge. Crysti's hands dove into a bowl of pretzels on the counter.

"How was it at your aunt's?" I asked as Amanda sat down across from me.

"Boring! I mean, really, I felt like a hostage or something! There's nothing for about thirteen miles but all these little houses that look identical to each other except that they're different colors. Aunt Grace has a yellow one. She said one time some strange guy was out there on the porch, trying to get his key to work, and it turned out he belonged in a yellow house on the next block."

Amanda was the only person I knew who could turn boredom into a good story. Even Crysti stood still to listen.

Amanda jumped up and switched on the radio. A Whitney Houston song came on, and she began dancing around the room. Crysti hesitated for only a moment. Then she was bouncing around and snapping her fingers, too. I watched them from my chair, wondering where they found so much pep.

"So did you swim today?" Amanda asked, when the commercial came on.

"Of course I swam. We've got that meet with Elyria next Monday. Larry said today he's still putting me in, even though I've been a little off the past week or two."

"How *is* Larry, by the way?" Amanda asked with a knowing wink. I was sorry his name had come up. Crysti cocked her head, eager to catch every word.

I sipped my Sprite and hoped I wasn't blushing. Larry was the junior coach of my swim team at the Y. I didn't have a crush on him exactly; he was eighteen, too old to ever notice me. But he was really cute. I couldn't help thinking about him sometimes, even though I knew it was dumb.

"Larry's okay," I said casually. "He's just fine."

"Is he the one with the blond hair?" Crysti asked. "I saw him when we dropped you off the other day. He waved and you turned real red."

"According to you, I'm always changing color, like one of those chameleon lizards," I muttered. Amanda looked puzzled, and I hurried to change the subject. "They timed me this morning, only Katie Rosario bumped into me and messed me up. Last week I was eight seconds faster."

"So are you worried about the race?" Amanda asked.

"Not really. I mean, no more than usual. I always get kind of knotted up right before the starting whistle."

"I love to swim and all, but I wouldn't want to work at it like you do," Amanda said. "It'd take all the fun out of it."

"It's a different kind of fun. You're on a team, you're practicing with a bunch of other kids. And you're kind of testing yourself, seeing what you'll be able to do."

"I guess," Amanda said, shaking her head. "It just sounds like work to me."

"Let's *do* something," Crysti broke in. "You guys want to walk down to the drugstore? Just to go somewhere?"

"Don't tell me you're bored again already," I groaned. "We just got here!"

"I'm not bored," Crysti said. "I just mean, who wants to sit around?"

"I do," I said. "It's awful out."

"Well," Amanda pointed out, "the drugstore's air-conditioned. How about it?"

"All right," I said reluctantly. "I suppose I'm outvoted."

I stood up slowly, but my dizziness had passed. Amanda shouted into the living room that we were leaving, and grabbed some more pretzels for the road. "Hey," she said suddenly. "What happened to your leg?" She pointed to a big purplish bruise on my left thigh, just below my shorts.

I touched the spot gingerly. "That's where Katie kicked me at swim practice," I said. "She really got me, didn't she?"

"I'll say," Amanda exclaimed. "That must hurt."

"What happened to you over here?" Crysti wanted to know. She was looking at a smaller bruise on my right calf.

"I don't even remember where that one came from," I said. "I never noticed it before."

Amanda walked around me, studying me from all angles. "You've got a black-and-blue mark on your elbow," she remarked, "and a little one on your ankle. Who's beating you up, anyway?"

"You got me," I said, laughing. "Who ever said swimming isn't a contact sport?"

Oberlin, Ohio, is a strange place to live. On the outskirts of most towns there are strip malls or big shopping centers, but if you walk too far on any of our main streets you'll get lost in a cornfield. There's nothing much here except a college. In August, with the students gone for summer vacation, the town hardly exists. The central square is deserted, and the stores around it have a dusty, sleepy expression, as though they don't know why they're open at all.

"Oberlin in the long hot summer," Crysti murmured. She paused, and I could tell she was making up a song.

"No other town is such a bummer," I suggested.

"Yeah, that's not bad," Crysti said. She hummed one line, then another, experimenting. "In two days you could die of boredom . . ."

"Nothing rhymes with *boredom*," I told her. "Now you're stuck."

Crysti thought for a while, scuffing her sandals through the grass. Suddenly her face brightened. "In two days you could die of boredom," she repeated. " 'Cause every day is more and more

9

dumb. Get it? Boredom — *more* dumb."

"Brilliant!" Amanda cried. "Take a bow!"

Crysti bowed, and we all applauded, and giggled the rest of the way to the store.

"Ah!" breathed Amanda as we pushed through the heavy glass doors. "This is how life was meant to be!"

A blast of cool air struck my face. The delicious freshness enveloped me, stroking my forehead, caressing my arms. The soles of my bare feet seemed to sigh with relief each time they touched the linoleum.

"Look at this!" Crysti called, holding up a package of fake fingernails about three inches long. "Do vampires shop in here or what?"

"I need a new bathing cap," I said. "My old one looks like somebody's dog chewed it up." Most of the girls on the swim team kept their hair short, because it was so much easier to take care of. But I liked mine long. It came down to the middle of my back, thick and shiny and so dark it was almost black. I needed an extra large bathing cap to contain it all.

We cruised the aisles, searching for anything interesting, for nothing at all. By now the suffocating heat outside was only a memory. In fact, I was actually starting to feel chilly.

In front of the Barbie dolls we ran into Iris Block from my class at school. Normally I tried

10

to avoid Iris. Amanda once said she had "the wrong remark for every occasion." But somehow it was fun to meet her there unexpectedly, in the middle of summer, when nothing surprising ever happened. Iris said she'd seen Mr. Nader, our principal, at McDonald's, yelling at his eight-year-old for squeezing catsup all over the table. It wasn't really very funny. But we all got to laughing so hard an old man gave us a weird look, and that made us laugh more than ever.

"Hey, Jill!" Iris said suddenly. "Who's been knocking you around?"

Self-consciously I clapped my hand over the bruise on my leg. But I couldn't hide the others, there were too many of them. "I got in a fight," I said. "I met a vampire with three-inch fingernails."

"Looks like you got the worst of it," Iris said. "Really, you look awful."

"Iris Block scores again," Amanda said as soon as she was out of earshot.

"What do you mean?" Crysti wanted to know. "What are you guys talking about?"

"Nothing," we said almost in unison. "Never mind." We could have let her in on the joke, I supposed. Still, I just didn't feel like explaining things to my little sister all the time. She didn't have to know *everything*.

"I almost wish I had a sweater," I said as we

turned down the next aisle. "They crank the air-conditioning up way too high in here, don't you think?"

Crysti looked at me, wrinkling her forehead. "It's impossible to be *too* chilly today," she declared. "I'm ready to move to the arctic."

"Well, I'm cold," I said. I rubbed my arms, but it didn't help.

"I don't believe it!" Amanda said. "You've actually got goose pimples!"

"It's my Mediterranean blood," I told her. "My Sicilian ancestors never experienced anything but sunshine."

"What about me?" Crysti demanded. "My ancestors are just as Sicilian as yours, don't forget."

"Cut it out," I said peevishly. "I'm just cold, okay? I can't help it."

"Okay, okay," Crysti said, backing away. "You don't have to get so mad."

"You guys quit the sibling rivalry," Amanda said. "This is neutral territory."

"It's *iceberg* territory," I grumbled. "I'm freezing to death."

Amanda wandered off to look at headbands, and I finally found a new green bathing cap with daisies on it. By the time we all met at the checkout line, I was shivering.

"Don't you love to read these?" Crysti asked, taking a copy of the *National Enquirer* from a rack by the door. " 'ALIENS TEACH INFANT

TO SING "THE STAR-SPANGLED BAN-NER." ' 'FOSSILIZED MERMAID DISCOV-ERED IN ARIZONA QUARRY.' 'CURE FOR LEUKEMIA COMES FROM AFRICAN COCKROACH.' "

"Yeah, right," I said, as the checkout girl slid my bag across the counter.

"Well, maybe a baby *could* sing 'The Star-Spangled Banner,' if it was a genius kid," Amanda said. "And you never know — there might have been something like a mermaid in ancient times, or else where did all the stories come from?"

I took the paper from Crysti and studied the headlines.

"Didn't you see the sign?" The checkout girl glared at me over the cash register. "It says 'No bare feet permitted in the store.' "

I glanced down guiltily and tried to conceal one foot under the other. "That's discrimination," Amanda protested. "Bare feet should be equal to feet with shoes on."

"Oh, let's go," I said as another wave of shivering seized me. "Let's just get out of here."

As I put the *Enquirer* back on the rack, I glimpsed the last line of the story: "Researchers claim that within a year all forms of leukemia will be eradicated."

"Too bad you can't believe everything you read," I remarked. "I bet they pay people to sit around all day and write that junk."

13

"Wouldn't that be a fun way to make a living?" Crysti mused. "I could do it, easy. 'TALKING MICE IMPORTED FROM INDIA.' 'WOMAN MEETS GHOST OF ABRAHAM LINCOLN.' "

We pushed out through the glass doors again. After the icy air in the store, the heat hit me harder than ever. My head began to throb, and I heard a steady pounding in my ears. "I've got to sit down," I said, and my voice sounded muffled.

Crysti and Amanda hovered around me, battering me with questions. "What's the matter? . . . Are you okay? . . . Do you feel sick?"

I took two stumbling steps toward a bench on the corner. Amanda caught my arm and helped me the last few feet.

"What *is* it?" she asked anxiously. "Your face looks — "

"I know," I said, struggling to laugh. "Pasty, right?" I put my head down on my knees the way I had before, and pretended to examine a line of ants marching along the ground. In a few moments I felt a little better.

"I bet you're working too hard," Amanda was saying beside me. "You spend too much time swimming laps. Maybe you should just take it easy sometimes."

Slowly, cautiously, I sat up straight. "Don't say anything to Dad," I warned Crysti. "You know how he's such a worrywart."

14

"Maybe you *ought* to say something, if you really don't feel good, Jill," Amanda said. "Maybe you should see a doctor or something."

I was starting to feel embarrassed. "It's no big deal," I said. "Going from hot to cold to hot — it kind of throws you. Give me another minute."

They waited patiently, standing at either side of me like a pair of royal guards. I sat for a long time, not talking much, watching the cars go by. Whenever I thought of getting up, a weight seemed to press down on my shoulders, holding me in place on the bench, and I'd decide to rest just a little longer.

On the bank across the street the minute hand jerked one notch forward, then another. Seven-twelve. Seven-thirteen. The thermometer boasted that it was eighty-nine degrees out, but it felt like one hundred and eighty-nine to me. If I sat here until the sun went down, the air might be cooler. But that was ridiculous. I couldn't tell Crysti and Amanda that I wanted to wait on a bench on College Street till the sun set.

All right, I told myself. When the clock said seven-fifteen, I would stand up.

A boy sped past on a bicycle. A little girl and her mother came out of Gibson's Bakery. The minute hand jerked and was still. Jerked once more.

With all my strength and willpower, I forced myself to my feet. Once I was up, with the earth firmly settled under me, I knew I could manage. My dizziness hadn't gone completely, but it was only a misty humming behind my thoughts.

"Okay, let's go," I said and began the long, hot journey home.

# 2

I always felt a little shaky when I woke up on the day of a swim meet. It was a combination of dread and excitement, a flutter in my stomach, an electric tingling all through me. I couldn't eat; I couldn't sit still; I couldn't wait to hear the starting whistle.

Monday morning, the day of the meet with Elyria, I was even more nervous than usual. For over a week my time had been falling off. I'd get winded after three laps and have to stop and rest. Mrs. Brownlow, our head coach, told me not to strain myself, to go at my own pace for a while and build myself back up gradually. So far her strategy hadn't worked. She and Larry had every reason to pull me out of the meet and put in one of the new kids, somebody who could really help the team. But they hadn't. They were still counting on me.

Crysti was already at the table when I got downstairs for breakfast. When I reached for the

17

Captain Crunch, she tugged the box out of my hand. "Let me finish!" she exclaimed. "I'm doing the maze!"

"Right," I grumbled. "I can starve, as long as you finish the maze on the cereal box."

"It's a little early for you two to start this up, isn't it?" Dad inquired from behind the newspaper. "Couldn't you wait till ten o'clock at least?"

Crysti dropped her pencil and pushed the box in my direction without looking at me. I poured half a bowlful, but I really wasn't hungry. Food was hardly worth fighting for this morning.

Mom had already left for work; she sold real estate from an office in Elyria. But Dad was home all summer. He taught history at the college, and spent the summers writing journal articles about the Civil War. Sometimes he said he drew his inspiration from watching the battles between Crysti and me. Even though he complained when we made too much noise, I liked having him around.

"What time do you have to be at the Y?" he asked me. "I assume you need a ride."

"Nine o'clock," I said. "Yeah, a ride'd be nice."

I scraped out my bowl and put it into the sink. I was turning to leave when Dad stopped me.

"Come here a minute," he said. "What'd you do to your arm?"

Obediently I held out my right arm for his inspection. His finger traced a big purple bruise just above the elbow. "I must have bumped into something," I said. "I don't remember."

"It looks gross," Crysti said cheerfully. "Worse than the ones you had the other night."

I edged toward the door, glad I had put on long pants today. I didn't want anyone to see the bruises that still decorated my legs.

But I wasn't going to escape. "Hey, look!" Crysti cried. "You've got one on your other arm, too. They match."

"Let me see." Dad got up and led me to the window, where he could study me in the sunlight. "They're pretty big," he remarked. "I should think you wouldn't forget whamming yourself that hard."

"I guess I'm getting clumsy lately," I said, laughing a little. "Everybody teases me about it. If there's an open door, I'll walk right into it."

Dad was still examining my arms. "It looks like you've got a rash of some kind," he remarked. "See this — all these little pinpricks?"

It was true. My forearm was speckled with reddish dots. I stared at them in amazement. When had they appeared? Why hadn't I noticed them when I got dressed this morning? I felt as if my own body had played a trick on me.

"Do they itch?" Dad asked.

I shook my head. "They don't feel like anything. I didn't even know they were there."

"Let me see," Crysti said, crowding in to get a

19

good look. "Wow! There's some on your neck, too. Like along your collarbone, up to your chin."

"Better have your mother take a good look tonight, see what she thinks," Dad said. "I'll bet you're allergic to something."

"I'll be late for the meet if I don't get going," I said. "I'll be back down in a second."

Normally I would have bounded upstairs to grab the blue canvas bag with my tank suit and my new bathing cap. But I was starting to get a headache, and I found myself moving more slowly than I intended. Upstairs I flopped onto my unmade bed, just for a moment. I held out one arm, then the other, and studied the strange new pattern of dots and bruises. Then I pushed up my pants cuffs and looked at my calves. The purple blotches Amanda had noticed last week hadn't gone away. If anything, they were bigger than ever. I wasn't kidding when I told Dad that everyone was teasing me lately. Just yesterday at swim practice, Katie Rosario said I looked like a boxer who had lost the championship.

It was nice to lie still, listening to the sounds of the house. A murmur of voices floated to me up the stairs, comfortable, contented, though the words were only a blur. The back door banged, and a moment later Crysti's bicycle bell clanged beneath my window.

"Jill?" Dad called. "You about ready?"

"Coming."

My head pounded resentfully as I sat up. I'd never be any good in the water if I felt like this. I hurried into the bathroom and gulped a Tylenol with a glass of water. In a few minutes I'd start to feel better, I assured myself. I slung my canvas bag over my shoulder and met Dad at the foot of the stairs.

"We should have taken your temperature," Dad said as he pulled into the Y parking lot. "That's the first question your mother'll ask me."

"I haven't got a fever," I insisted. "You don't get a fever from allergies, do you?"

"Probably not. But she's going to ask me, anyhow."

I pushed open my door and stepped out. "Thanks for the ride, Dad," I said. "Don't worry — I'm okay."

"Good luck with your race," Dad said. "Give me a call when you're through — I'll be home."

The heat wave had finally broken, and the air was fresh and breezy as I crossed the parking lot to the locker-room entrance. Inside was the usual hubbub — our team clustered over on the right, the girls from Elyria by themselves on the other side, everyone talking at once. Cindy McGrath had a boom box pumping out a rap song. The Tylenol hadn't taken effect; with that amount of noise it never would. In TV interviews I'd heard professional athletes talk about "working straight through the pain." That was what I'd have to do this morning.

As I changed into my suit, I cast a doleful glance at the mirror. The rash was starting to come up on my thighs, too — the same dusting of red dots that ornamented my arms. Maybe I was getting chickenpox, or scarlet fever. I'd already had one of them, but I couldn't remember which.

I draped a towel over my shoulder to hide as much of myself as I could, and headed for the pool. Larry and the other junior coach, Sue, gathered us together for a last-minute pep talk. "Elyria's got a strong team," Sue warned us. "They were in the state finals last year. But all of you have been working hard this summer, and you're ready for a challenge. You people can *do* it."

"Don't think about their record," Larry added. "Just think about yourselves, think about winning."

Sue glanced down at her clipboard. "Here's your lineup," she announced. "Katie Rosario, lane one. Cindy McGrath, lane two. Jill Marino, you're in lane three . . . "

I took my place at the side of the pool and waited. My head pounded, my stomach lurched. But once I hit the water I'd be all right, I'd be moving, doing what I had to do. Voices and laughter echoed around me, bouncing from the high domed ceiling. I poised on the balls of my feet as Sue counted down: "Three, two, one . . . " and the blast of the starting whistle ripped the air.

It must have been a tremendous splash — eight girls diving in at the same precise moment. But I didn't really notice it. I felt the shock of the cold water rising up around me, closing over my head; then I was up again, striking out with long, fierce strokes.

Just ahead of me I saw a pair of feet, kicking with a steady, determined rhythm. My body felt oddly heavy, a cumbersome weight as I pulled it through the water. I touched the far side of the pool and started back, but my arms ached with the effort, my kick grew weaker. Each time I lifted my face to breathe, I couldn't seem to gulp in enough air.

I was losing my rhythm. My strokes became choppy and desperate, as though I were a helpless beginner. I remember glancing up and marveling that the edge of the pool was still far away, though I had been swimming toward it for hours.

This was a meet, I reminded myself sternly. I had to compete, drive ahead, put the other swimmers behind me.

If I could only rest a little, then I could catch up. I stretched my toes toward the bottom, to stand, to catch my breath just for a moment. But I reached down and down through endless water. Yes, I remembered, it was nine feet here at the deep end, below the high dive.

There would be no rest. I would keep moving,

stroke upon stroke, pushing past yards and feet and inches until I could feel the solid rim of the pool under my fingers.

But I couldn't stop there. Nobody stopped in the middle of a race. No . . . I would have to keep on . . . until the finish. . . .

Again my feet searched uselessly for the tiled bottom. For a minute the water held me suspended, head up, and I sucked in a great lungful of air. Dimly I heard another whistle, and I thought, I've blown it, the race is over and here I am, what will Larry say. . . .

"Jill! Jill! It's all right, I've got you!" It was Mrs. Brownlow's voice, close to my shoulder. I struggled against a pair of arms that wanted to drag me under again.

"Hold still," she said. "I've got you."

Piece by appalling piece, my mind absorbed the truth. The race had come to a halt. Katie and Cindy peered at me wide-eyed from the side of the pool. Larry stood by with a couple of towels, and Sue stared in frightened disbelief. Mrs. Brownlow drew me along through the water, caught the rim, and held my head above the surface as Larry hoisted me out of the pool.

Hunched on the wet concrete, I coughed helplessly. Someone wrapped me in warm, dry towels, but I was shivering and I couldn't stop.

"What happened?" Sue asked. "Did you have a cramp?"

Another fit of coughing took hold of me. When it was finally over, I could barely speak. "No," I managed. "I just — kind of — "

"It looked like she passed out," said the coach from Elyria, a tall, skinny guy with thinning hair. "I saw she was having trouble, starting to flounder. And then she went down like a rock!"

"Should we call an ambulance?" Larry asked.

"No!" I cried. "Please — I'm all right now!"

"Listen to that," Sue said with relief. "She *must* be feeling better."

Maybe an ambulance wasn't such a bad idea, I thought grimly. An ambulance that would whisk me away from all these anxious, curious faces. I wanted to disappear, to slip beyond the reach of questions. I had ruined the race. They had hauled me out, half-drowned, and they would never want me on the team again. I was a loser, a disgrace.

"Go in and put some dry clothes on," Mrs. Brownlow decided. "Are your parents home? Is there someone who can pick you up?"

"My dad." I rose unsteadily, pulling the towel more tightly around me.

"Sue, go in with her," Mrs. Brownlow said. "Just in case."

I shrank with shame under the words. Just in case what? In case I collapsed on the floor? In case I was too weak to dress myself? I'd never live down this morning — never!

Obediently Sue walked beside me, slowing her

steps to mine. "I fainted once," she said. "I was singing in church, and it was about a hundred degrees up in the choir loft, and all of a sudden *boom!* There I was flat out, with everybody leaning over me, putting wet washcloths on my forehead! It was the most embarrassing thing that ever happened to me."

"I know," I said. "I could just die! I mean it! I could just curl up someplace and die!"

"It won't seem so awful tomorrow," Sue assured me. "Nothing ever does."

"Maybe. But right now, I wish I'd never have to see anybody here again."

Tomorrow, I thought, pulling my clothes out of my locker. Tomorrow this would all be behind me. And someday, after a whole pile of tomorrows, I would laugh about it. About the day I practically drowned in the middle of a race and almost gave my coach a heart attack.

Tomorrow had to be better than today.

# 3

Dad picked me up at the Y, looking mildly worried. He asked me if I'd been eating enough, if I'd been pushing myself too hard with the swimming practices, if I was upset about anything. Yes, I said, I was plenty upset, I'd looked like a total jerk in front of everybody. But he said that wasn't what he meant. He wanted to know if I was under too much stress. "When you get stressed out, it can make your body do strange things," he explained. "If you don't know when to stop, your body puts the brakes on for you."

"I've been having a great summer," I protested. "I *like* swimming. It doesn't make me feel sick."

"You could just have a bug," Dad said. "Better take it easy for a while."

I didn't argue about that. As soon as we got home, I climbed the stairs to my room and sank onto my bed. Before I dropped off to sleep, I heard Dad downstairs, setting up an appointment with Dr. Lewis.

Even then, I really wasn't scared. Being sick meant having the flu, or maybe a strep throat — something that would be uncomfortable for a while and would eventually go away. Mom would plump up my pillows and bring me meals on a tray, and Crysti would come in to distract me with the silly songs she was always making up. In a day or two, I'd be on my feet again. I would forget that anything had ever gone wrong.

As soon as Mom got home from work, she hurried upstairs to see me and take my temperature. "One-oh-one," she reported. "You've got a touch of something, that's for sure. Let me see your arms. Your father tells me you've got a rash."

By now the red speckles had swept up past my elbows and crept down my neck across my chest. Here and there the pinpricks were crowded out by big purple splotches. Mom pulled down the covers and looked at my legs. The bruise where Katie had kicked me sprawled across my thigh like a big misshapen saucer.

Mom drew the covers up again and tucked them close around me, the way she used to when I was little. She stood looking at me a minute, frowning.

"How come I feel so cold if I've got a fever?" I asked. "I start to go to sleep and I wake up shivering."

"I don't know," Mom said, shaking her head. "There are a lot of things I just don't know."

It made me a little uneasy, to hear her say that.

I guess I still expected my parents to have all the answers. But I wasn't worried. All I had to do was wait for tomorrow.

Sure enough, I felt a bit better when I awoke the next morning. I still had the rash, but my headache and chills were gone. I dressed and headed downstairs for breakfast. In the kitchen doorway I stopped short. Mom stood at the counter, slicing an orange.

"Aren't you going to be late?" I asked. "You have a closing this morning, don't you?"

"I called in. Pat will go for me," she explained. "Your father and I both want to go with you to the doctor."

"You don't *both* need to come," I protested. "It's no big deal."

"Probably not," she said briskly. "But I've got a couple of questions. I think it'd be a good idea for both of us to go."

Parents take their kids to the doctor all the time, I reminded myself. Fathers, mothers, any combination.

As if she read my mind, Mom added, "It's part of the job description, you know — the contract parents have to sign." She turned away with a tight little laugh and gazed out the window over the sink. I had the feeling that she and Dad had stayed up last night having a long talk. A long talk about me.

That was the moment, the very first moment, when I truly began to feel frightened.

My appointment was scheduled for eleven, but as usual Dr. Lewis's waiting room overflowed with people who were there ahead of me. Most of his patients were pudgy babies in for shots, or toddlers who kept scrambling away from their mothers and trying to escape into the hall. I was by far the oldest kid there. If any of my friends could have peeked in the door and seen me, I would have been mortally embarrassed. There I sat, amid the Legos and Tinkertoys, with Mickey Mouse posters and little kids' crayon drawings covering the walls.

"Aren't I old enough to go to a regular doctor?" I grumbled. "Just because I started out as a baby, do I have to see a pediatrician for the rest of my life?"

"It makes sense to see somebody who knows you," Mom said. "Dr. Lewis has all your records."

Resignedly I picked up a copy of *Highlights* magazine. There was nothing to do but wait.

It was almost noon when the receptionist finally called my name. "Room six," she said, pointing down the hall. Dad stayed in the waiting room, but Mom came into the examining room with me.

Dr. Lewis's nurse, Gloria, was there to meet us. She never changed; as far back as I could remember, she had always been plump and gray-haired and smiling, with a little too much rouge on her cheeks. "I just want to check your height and weight before the doctor comes in," she explained. "Take your shoes off and step on the scale for me, all right?"

Gloria's voice was gently reassuring. All my life, every time I'd come in for school checkups or camp physicals, for sprains or sore throats, she said the same words. This was just one more routine appointment, I told myself. Probably I didn't need to be here at all.

I stepped onto the scale.

"Keep your feet still," Gloria said. "There, all set." She picked up my folder from the doctor's desk and wrote down today's figures. "You been dieting, Jill?" she asked suddenly. "You've lost seven pounds since the last time you were here."

"That was when?" Mom asked. "March?"

"March fourteenth. She had a bad cough, remember?"

"Seven pounds," Mom mused. "That's quite a bit, isn't it? In such a short time?"

Gloria didn't answer. "Change into your gown," she told me. "The doctor will be right in. You can discuss everything with him." She backed away and slipped out the door, almost as though she were in retreat.

I got into the stiff cotton gown and sat on a plastic chair, so low that my knees came almost to my chin. Before I had time to get uncomfortable, Dr. Lewis opened the door. "Jill Marino," he said. "What brings you in here on such a nice summer day?"

"We're not sure if it's an allergy or some funny virus," Mom broke in before I could say a word. "She's got a rash all over her, and some very large purplish marks. And she's running a bit of a fever. Yesterday she seems to have fainted — we weren't with her, she was swimming at the Y, but they tell us she passed out — "

"I didn't," I interrupted. "I knew what was going on. I got tired is all."

Dr. Lewis gave me his full attention. He was so pale he looked as if he hadn't stepped outside his office since Memorial Day. He must work hard, I thought, remembering that squalling mob in the waiting room. Maybe that was why he had such a tired, frowning expression as he asked, "What can you tell me, Jill? What's been bothering you?"

"Nothing much, really," I said. "Once in a while I get these headaches that are kind of bad. And I've got a weird rash, like Mom told you. And — " I hesitated. "I get so cold. Once I get chilly it seems like I can't warm up again, and I just sit and shiver."

"Let's take a look at your rash." Dr. Lewis lifted my arms and studied each in turn. He pushed aside the cotton gown and examined me from head to toe, as I shuddered with a wretched blend of cold and humiliation. Gingerly he touched the biggest bruise, the one on my left leg. "That hurt?" he asked.

"A little," I said. "Mostly it just looks ugly."

"Lie back," he ordered. I stretched out on the crinkling paper coverlet, and he poked and probed under my ribs, as though he were searching for something. Whatever it was, I prayed he wouldn't find it.

At last Dr. Lewis folded the gown over me again. "Sit up, and let's have a look in your mouth," he said. "Wider. There. Do your gums bleed when you brush your teeth?"

"Yeah, I guess so," I said uneasily. "Don't everybody's?"

"Do they bleed other times, too? For no reason?"

"I don't know. Maybe. I suppose so. Once in a while." I had the feeling I was giving away a secret. Dr. Lewis was gathering up clues, piecing them together. I didn't want him to show me the final picture.

Slowly, relentlessly, the examination went on. "Tilt your head back a little," Dr. Lewis ordered. His icy fingers slid up and down my neck, pausing here and there, then moving on again.

"What do you think the problem is?" Mom asked from her chair in the corner.

"It could be a virus," Dr. Lewis said, poking under my chin. "It could be a number of things. We won't really know what we're dealing with here until we do some blood work."

"A blood test!" I cried, sitting bolt upright. "That's when they stick you, right? I hate that! Do I have to have one?"

"I'm afraid so," Dr. Lewis said, pulling open a drawer in his supply cabinet. "It's nothing. Just a little mosquito bite."

I was too old to make a fuss about a little prick with a needle. But somehow today I couldn't face it. Today it was too much, more than I could bear.

Dr. Lewis swabbed the inside of my elbow, searching for a vein. I winced away from the coldness of the alcohol on my skin. "You've got to hold nice and still," he said, a note of sternness creeping into his voice.

Mom stepped to my side and took my hand. "Squeeze as hard as you can," she told me.

"Like that?" I asked. I gripped her hand as hard as I could, still never taking my eyes off Dr. Lewis. He had the needle in his hand, it swooped toward my unprotected skin. "No!" I cried, but it was too late. The needle stabbed into my arm, and Dr. Lewis held it in place as the vial filled with my blood, drop by slow red drop.

"That wasn't so bad, was it?" he asked, extracting the needle at last. It was an automatic question, the kind that didn't expect a response.

But there was nothing automatic about Mom's question. She wanted an answer, right now. "What do you think?" she asked as Dr. Lewis patted a Band-Aid into place. "Could she be allergic to something? Allergies can have some very strange symptoms, can't they?"

Dr. Lewis glanced around the room, as though he were looking for a way out. "It's too soon to know anything, really," he said, not looking at either one of us. "When we get the blood work back from the lab, we'll know more."

"But you must have some ideas," Mom prodded. "You're looking for specific things."

"Well — " Dr. Lewis stared at a picture beside the door, a toothy dinosaur in bright purple crayon. "It could be a whole range of things. There's no use going into the possibilities at this stage. We'll have some answers by tomorrow morning."

"My husband is out in the waiting room," Mom said. "I think he has some questions, too."

"All right," Dr. Lewis said, backing toward the door. "Jill, you get dressed and wait out there while I talk a minute with your mom and dad."

I don't remember getting dressed again, or walking back down the hall. I barely heard the waiting room squealing and banging around me. I sat alone on a stiff vinyl couch, while Mom and Dad and Dr. Lewis talked over my body's odd, troubling behavior, while they counted up the possibilities and weighed them one by one. Why didn't Dr. Lewis simply pat my shoulder and write out a prescription for an antibiotic? What were they saying to each other, behind the closed door of room six?

Suddenly I had to know.

I got to my feet and stepped around four-year-old twin girls, absorbed in a noisy tug-of-war over a one-legged Barbie doll. The receptionist was on the phone, and she never glanced my way as I slipped through the door. My heart pounding, I tiptoed down the hall toward the murmur of voices. The door was open a crack, just wide enough to let Dad's words find their way out to me.

"She's always been perfectly healthy," he was saying. "Now, if it was Crystal, our other one — she comes down with everything. She's a magnet for every cold germ in town." It was Dad's voice, but it didn't sound like Dad. The words came too fast, a jumbled frantic rush.

"You'll call us by noon tomorrow?" Mom asked. "Really, I don't know how we'll manage this. Just getting through the next twenty-four hours — "

"As I said," Dr. Lewis broke in, "there are a number of fairly benign blood disorders . . . "

A door burst open further down the hall, and a smiling mother emerged with a little boy in a Batman sweatshirt. He grinned at me and held up his lollipop.

". . . wrong to dwell on the worst-case scenario," Dr. Lewis's voice went on. I had missed something somewhere. What *was* the worst-case scenario? "I had a patient last year, very similar symptoms — turned out he had mononucleosis."

*Mononucleosis.* I rolled the word around in my mind, trying to remember where I'd heard it before. It sounded awful, whatever it was. And Dr. Lewis was trying to cheer everybody up, saying I might *only* have that. Just mononucleosis. Instead of . . .

"My dog has three puppies," the little boy announced. "Wanna see them?"

I shook my head. ". . . wondering what we should tell her," Mom's voice came through, thin and worried. "She's more anxious than she looks, I think. She'll want to know . . . "

The little boy marched up to me and stopped, his hands on his hips. "You *don't* want to see them?" he demanded. "They won't bite you. You could come to my house. My mom'd let you."

"Paul!" his mother said sharply. "We have to go pick up your sister."

"Maybe tomorrow," Paul called back as she hurried him away. "Maybe some day."

The distraction was just enough to throw me off guard. I must have missed some cue, some telltale rustle inside the room that would have warned me in time. Suddenly the door swung wide, and Dad stared out at me. "Jill!" he exclaimed. "What are you doing here? You're supposed to be in the — "

"How long have you been out here?" Mom

squeezed her way past him and studied me face-to-face. "You were listening, weren't you?"

"Don't I have a right to know what's going on?" I flared. "Who's all this about, anyway? It concerns me more than anybody else — I *ought* to listen."

"There's probably nothing to get upset about," Dr. Lewis said somewhere behind me. "We're not keeping secrets. But we don't want you to be alarmed for nothing."

"As soon as we know anything for sure, of course we'll explain everything to you," Mom went on, herding me back toward the receptionist's desk. "No one's deliberately keeping you in the dark."

"Yeah, right," I said. But it wasn't fair. They had no right to leave me in the waiting room with the babies while they had their conference without me. I was thirteen, old enough to understand whatever was going on. I'd make them explain from the beginning, fill in all the blanks.

But all the way home in the car Mom and Dad were quiet, together in the front seat. I sat by myself in back, watching the streets glide past the window, and I never asked what Dr. Lewis meant by "the worst-case scenario."

# 4

I never knew you could wake up tired after sleeping all night long. But that's what happened to me the next morning. I staggered down to breakfast, nibbled at a slice of toast, and stretched out on the living-room couch wrapped in an afghan. Crysti put on the TV, then got bored and wandered outside. Some kiddie show came on, with a clown handing out prizes, and I didn't have the energy to change the channel.

Far away, out in the kitchen, the phone rang. I heard the murmur of Dad's voice, but I couldn't understand any words. Within a few moments the receiver clicked back into place.

Then I heard the silence. It crept like some dark, scaly creature without legs, twisting around corners, gliding from room to room until it filled the whole house. Even the chatter of the TV seemed remote, part of another time.

I sat up, the afghan tumbling to the floor. "Dad?" I asked. "Who was that?"

His steps crossed the kitchen, drawing closer. But he didn't reply.

"Dad?" I called, raising my voice. "Who was on the phone?"

He stood in the doorway, leaning against it as if he needed something to hold him up. But when he spoke, his voice was surprisingly steady. "That was Dr. Lewis. We have to see him this afternoon at one o'clock. He wants to talk to us."

"Can't he just explain over the phone?" I asked. "When I had a throat culture that time, they just gave us the results — "

"I think," Dad said slowly, "that this is a little more complicated."

Mom, Dad, and I walked into Dr. Lewis's together. The waiting room was as crowded as usual, but Gloria told us to go straight to room six. As we stepped into the hall, a woman's voice behind me demanded, "Why is he taking *them?* We've been waiting since twelve!"

"Sometimes there are emergencies," Gloria explained, and shut the door firmly behind us.

Why was I an emergency today? I wondered. I was just as tired yesterday; I had just as many bruises. Yesterday I had to wait for over an hour.

In the office, I waited for Gloria to make some perky remark about seeing me so often. But she only said, "The doctor will be right with you," and backed out the door.

Mom sank onto a hard-looking wooden chair, and Dad paced up and down the tiny room. I perched on the little plastic chair again, with my knees up to my chin.

Dr. Lewis came in on a wave of apologies. "Sorry to keep you," he began, though we'd only been waiting for a few moments.

He went to his desk and riffled through a stack of folders. At last he found the one he wanted. He studied it for a long time before he spoke again. "Maybe it might be better — " He hesitated, glanced at me, and looked away again. "I think Jill ought to wait outside while I talk to the two of you together."

"No!" I cried. "I'm not a baby! You've got to tell me what's going on!"

"She'll have to know," Mom said wearily. "I don't believe in hiding things."

"Yes," Dr. Lewis said, "that generally is the best attitude. Keep everything out in the open." He turned a page, then another.

"You have the results of the blood tests?" Dad prodded.

Dr. Lewis put down the folder. He turned and faced us. "They came in this morning," he said. "Her white count is 98,000."

"What does that mean?" Mom asked.

"Well it's abnormally elevated — very high, in other words; and her platelets are way down, only 60,000. Ordinarily it ought to be anywhere from

150,000 to about 450,000. That's what's causing the bruises. When the platelets are low, you get a lot of bleeding under the skin."

"What does all this mean?" Dad demanded. "What do they tell us, all these figures?"

"Nothing yet, nothing for certain. We just don't know for sure. We'll need some more blood work. And a bone marrow, that's the most conclusive test. She'll have to go into the hospital, and they can get everything done right away."

"The *hospital!*" I cried. "Why? Tests for *what?*"

"We're not sure yet," Mom said, putting a soothing hand on my arm. "We're trying to find out — "

"Find out *what?* You're not telling me!"

I saw Mom and Dad look at one another. I couldn't read their long, wordless glance, but I knew they were speaking back and forth. At last Dad turned to Dr. Lewis and nodded.

Dr. Lewis became very intent on his hands. He cupped them together as though they held something precious and fragile.

"What's going on?" I repeated. "It's about me! I've got a right to know!"

Dr. Lewis spread his hands before him, wide and empty. "I'm afraid," he said, "there's a chance — just a possibility — that you may have leukemia."

*Leukemia.* It had such a gentle, delicate sound, like a girl's name. Some lovely, exotic young woman with wind-tossed hair, beckoning from a thicket of willows.

*Leukemia.* The girl shifted, melted away, and I saw a clawed hand stretch toward me, the fingers opening and closing, ready to seize me and drag me down. . . .

"I don't have *that!*" I was on my feet, staring wildly around me. "I've got the flu, that's all. I'm getting over it already. I feel fine!"

"I hope it's something simple," Dr. Lewis sighed. "You may have mononucleosis. The symptoms can be very similar. Mono is no fun, but basically it just means you'll have to rest for the next few weeks. That's the only treatment, just lots of rest."

"I can't rest for the next few weeks! I've got to swim!"

"Let's not worry about that yet," Dr. Lewis said. "Let's take it step by step."

I had sat in this office so many times, as far back as I could remember. Dr. Lewis stitched up my chin when I fell playing "Red Rover, Red Rover." He gave me an Ace bandage the day I sprained my ankle skating. Everything looked the same today — the little examining table for babies, the long one where I had lain yesterday, even the purple dinosaur by the door.

"We'll have to put her in the hospital this afternoon," Dr. Lewis said, talking straight past me. "Memorial up in Cleveland has a top-notch program. I called this morning — they have a bed ready."

"You mean we should go over there today?" Mom asked. "Now?"

"We don't want to lose any time," Dr. Lewis said. "The sooner we get to the bottom of this, the better."

He wrote something on a slip of paper and handed it to Dad. "She'll be seeing Dr. Carlos Echevarria," he explained. "He's one of the leading hematologists in the Midwest."

"Right now? This afternoon?" Mom said again. "We have to drive to Cleveland?"

"I know this is a shock," Dr. Lewis said. "Don't think ahead if you can help it. Just one thing at a time. Right now, make whatever arrangements you need, and get Jill into the hospital."

"I'll have to call my sister," Mom said, almost to herself. "Crysti can go over there for a few hours."

"A few hours!" Dad exclaimed. "By the time we get into the city, and find out what's going on, and — who knows how long — "

Their voices clattered around me. They were throwing words to each other, tossing them past me like tennis balls. I was eavesdropping again, listening in as they settled my life.

"Can we stay there overnight?" Dad wanted to know. "They let parents do that nowadays, don't they?"

"Memorial is very good that way," Dr. Lewis assured him. "They really encourage parents to be involved."

The patter of words went on and on, back and forth, back and forth, and at last Mom said we should go home and pack the things we'd need. "Come on, honey," she said, and took my hand. "Don't worry, everything's going to be all right."

I only nodded. There was nothing to say.

"How are you feeling?" Mom asked as I huddled in the backseat on the drive home. "Is the air-conditioning too much?"

"I'm okay," I said. "How long do I have to stay in the hospital, anyway?"

"I don't know," Mom said. "I guess we didn't ask, did we?"

"I don't think I heard one word out of ten that guy said in there," Dad muttered from behind the wheel. "I just blanked out."

"It's only a possibility," Mom insisted. "Dr. Lewis has always been thorough. He's just being extra careful."

Now I knew what they'd been discussing yesterday, when I stood outside the door. I knew what they meant by "the worst-case scenario." It was a girl with dark streaming hair — it was a skeleton hand, clawing toward me — it was leukemia.

# 5

The instant we got home from Dr. Lewis's office, Dad picked up the phone to begin a string of quick, urgent calls, leaving messages, canceling plans, making arrangements. Mom flew upstairs and threw things into overnight bags, one for me and one for the two of them. Then she rushed down the street and dragged Crysti home from the Shermans'. Crysti was still protesting when they banged through the front door, "But we were having so much *fun!* Why can't I just stay over there with Linda Sue?"

"We don't know how long we're going to be," Mom tried to explain. "You can stay at Aunt Cynthia's as long as you need to. It might be a couple of days."

Crysti must have been so stunned she forgot to argue. She hardly said another word until we were all packed into the car.

"Why can't I just come to the hospital with you guys?" she demanded as we pulled onto the highway. "How come I have to stay all by myself?"

"You won't exactly be by yourself," Mom said coaxingly. "You'll have your cousins to play with over there."

"Carla's bossy, and Eric won't play with me. I don't want to stay at Aunt Cynthia's!"

"Crysti!" Mom said sharply. "We've got enough to contend with right now! Just cooperate."

Crysti stared out the back window. We drove on in silence until we reached the turnoff. Then she started up again. "You still haven't told me why!"

"We're taking your sister to the hospital," Dad said from behind the wheel. "This is an emergency."

There it was again, that word *emergency*. A whirlwind had sprung up, engulfing everyone around me, and I was at its center. It mattered — mattered deeply — what happened to me. I had never felt quite so important before.

"You *told* me that part," Crysti said. "You *didn't* tell me what's the matter with her."

"It may be something pretty serious," Dad said. "We're going to the hospital to find out."

It wasn't true. I didn't have it — that disease Dr. Lewis named from behind his desk. I wouldn't say it, not even inside my own head. I might have something "pretty serious," but there were still questions, still chances for escape. Dr. Lewis could be on the wrong track. We were going up to Cleveland to get things straight, to find out the truth.

Crysti looked grim when we dropped her off at Aunt Cynthia's, but she didn't make a fuss. I thought we might go in for a minute and say hello to everyone. But Aunt Cynthia came out to the car and kissed Mom through the rolled-down window. "We'll take good care of her," she promised. "However long you need to be away."

"Thanks," Mom said, wiping her eyes. "We'll call . . . as soon as we know anything."

Aunt Cynthia walked around to my side of the car and leaned in to give me a hug. She smelled like geraniums, as if she had been working in the garden. "How you doing, kiddo?" she asked. "You don't look all that sick to me."

"I'm okay I guess," I said. Everything was happening so fast, I wasn't quite sure how I felt.

"Well, keep your spirits up," Aunt Cynthia said, giving my shoulder a parting pat. "Mind over matter, that's half the battle."

"Sure," I said. "I know."

Crysti climbed out slowly and stood on the sidewalk, clutching the bag with her nightgown and toothbrush. "Good-bye!" she shouted as the car pulled away.

" 'Bye," I called back, and tried to send her an encouraging smile. When we rounded the corner at the end of the block, she still stood on the curb, waving after us.

Dr. Lewis had told us to go straight to Admitting. But there was nothing straight about it. At first I trailed after Mom and Dad as they zigzagged through the white hospital corridors, but I was too exhausted to keep up with them. Finally Mom sat with me on a bench while Dad chased here and there, filling out forms.

"Dr. Lewis didn't make us wait like this," I said. "I guess here they have so many emergencies they don't even notice."

"It feels like such a long time ago," Mom said, gazing down at her lap, "being in Dr. Lewis's office . . ."

A nurse passed us, pushing a girl in a wheelchair. I knew it was rude to stare, but I couldn't help watching them. The girl's face had a puffed, sickly look. But the worst part, the thing that caught my gaze and wouldn't let me tear it away, was her hair. It was completely gone. Her head was as smooth as a Ping-Pong ball.

Middle-aged men went bald, and made jokes about how the floor is the best thing to stop falling hair. But this was a girl, a girl who must have been fifteen or sixteen. I wondered how she could venture out in public, even for a roll down the corridor with a nurse. Then for an instant our eyes met. She locked her gaze on mine with a look of challenge, as if she were daring me to stare at her, to put her down.

"Mom?" I whispered as the girl disappeared into

an elevator, "what's wrong with her?"

Before she could answer, Dad hurried toward us with a pile of papers in his hand. "We go up to the seventh floor and give all this stuff to the charge nurse," he announced. "Then she'll take us to the room."

It sounded simple enough, but the first elevator we found only went as far as the fourth floor. Almost too tired to stand, I tottered through the maze — back down to the lobby, along endless hallways jammed with carts and empty wheelchairs and orderlies with trays, up another elevator, and through a set of folding doors marked, PEDIATRIC ONCOLOGY. "This must be it," Dad said, stopping before a curved counter. "You have a bed for my daughter?"

If they didn't, I would have to curl up on the linoleum. I couldn't take another step. As Dad negotiated with the nurse, my legs folded and I slid to the floor, my back against the wall.

"Jill?" Mom hovered above me. "Are you all right?"

I smiled up at her. "If I was, I guess we wouldn't be here."

One nurse was still busy giving Dad papers to sign, but a second one emerged around the end of the counter. She wasn't much taller than I was, but she boosted me to my feet as though I were a doll. "This way, love," she said with a distinct

British accent. "Right to your room. Seven-oh-eight."

Room 708 was divided by a white curtain that hung from the ceiling. There was a wooden nightstand, a TV bolted high on the wall, and a bed with metal rails like a crib. The short British nurse, who said her name was Barbara, whisked me into a light cotton hospital gown with ties up the back, and helped me slip between the cool, crisp sheets.

"Dr. Echevarria will be in to see you tonight," she explained. "After the tests he'll probably order a transfusion, and you'll feel better in no time. Right now I'm going to start an IV."

I was so tired that I barely flinched when she stuck a needle into the back of my hand and taped it into place with adhesive. A thin, clear plastic tube wound from my hand to a bottle that dangled from a rack at the foot of my bed. I wondered vaguely what they were pouring into me, but I was too exhausted to care.

From the other side of the curtain, someone coughed. It was the sort of cough that was meant to attract attention. "Oh," Mom said brightly, "it looks like you've got a roommate."

"Yes," said Barbara, pushing the curtain aside. "Let me introduce you two. Elizabeth, you have company. This is the new girl on the ward — Jill Marino."

"Hi," said Elizabeth. "This your first time?"

"Yeah." My voice came out in a squeak. I couldn't find another word to say. Elizabeth was the girl I had seen downstairs — the girl without any hair.

Maybe Elizabeth thought I was being unfriendly. But I didn't care. I just couldn't hold my head up any longer, couldn't keep my eyes open. Somewhere in the twilight as I tumbled into sleep, I saw myself running, running with wings on my feet. Panting at my heels was a girl whose laughter cackled with malice, a girl with a shining bald head.

I wasn't allowed to sleep for long. In moments, it seemed, Mom's voice pulled me out of my fitful dream. "Jill," she called, "the doctor is here to see you."

Above me floated a smiling, bespectacled face. A broad male hand smoothed my covers. "Hi," said a stranger's voice. "I'm Dr. Echevarria. I want to explain a few things to you and your folks. Can you sit up for a minute?"

"I guess so," I said, without much enthusiasm.

"Good. This is how your bed works." He pointed to a button on the metal frame. "Push that, and see what happens."

I pressed the button obediently. From somewhere beneath me came a low hum, and the head of my bed lifted until I was propped in an almost normal sitting position.

"Pretty neat, huh?" asked Dr. Echavarria. He sounded as delighted as if he'd invented the gadget himself.

I gave a polite nod, and wondered when they would let me lie down again.

"Okay, this is what's happening," the doctor continued. "We have to do some tests to find out just what kind of sickness you have. That way we'll know which medicines will help you get better. You follow me?"

"Sure," I said. Dr. Lewis's guesses didn't mean a thing here. This big shot at Memorial would find out what I really had. He'd call up Dr. Lewis and say, "Don't do that to any more of your patients, you hear me! Don't scare any more kids for nothing. That girl had the flu all the time!"

"What kind of tests?" I asked.

"The nurse is going to take some blood from you, so we can study it very carefully. And tomorrow morning we need to look at a bit of your bone marrow."

The words snapped me wide awake. "At *what?*"

"The marrow inside your bones. You see, the bone marrow is where your blood cells are manufactured. So to find out what's happening with your blood, we need to get a good look at — "

"No way!" I exclaimed. "You're not going to cut into my bones! Forget it."

Mom came around to stand next to Dr. Echevarria. "You'll have a local anesthetic, they told me," she said. "It doesn't hurt."

"Where's Dad?" I asked suddenly. "He won't let them do this to me."

"I'm right here," Dad said, appearing in the doorway. "They *have* to do it, Jill. It's a matter of — a matter of — " He let the sentence dangle.

"Okay — so they do this test on me tomorrow," I said. "Can it prove I haven't got — you know — what Dr. Lewis said I might have?"

"Leukemia?" Dr. Echevarria said it so casually, as if it were just an ordinary word. "It will show us whether you have leukemia or some other blood disease. We can't start treating you until we know what the problem is."

Dr. Echevarria was actually taking a small-town baby doctor seriously. He was going to look for all the horrible things Dr. Lewis claimed I might have. Somehow I would prove they were all wrong. I'd make them look ridiculous — all these doctors who thought they knew so much.

The doctor talked on and on about the "procedure" I would have tomorrow. It was "relatively painless," he assured me, and "really quite routine." "Ask your roommate over there," he said, waving toward the drawn curtain. "Elizabeth can tell you. There's nothing to it, right, Liz?"

"Right," came Elizabeth's disembodied voice. "I've had about ten of them so far. It's no sweat."

"Hear that?" Dr. Echevarria said. "It sounds awful, but it's really not so bad."

They were all acting parts in some weird made-for-TV movie. I wished I could flip a switch and turn them off.

"Can I go to sleep now?" I asked. "I'm so tired I can't stand it."

"Sure," Dr. Echevarria said. "You might as well take it easy till the nurse comes in for your blood."

I reached out and pressed the magic button. With its low hum, my bed settled slowly back into its normal position. I closed my eyes. I could still escape. I could flee from all of them, into my dreams.

# 6

"**G**ood morning, Jill. Ready for breakfast?"
I pried my eyes open to discover a plump nurse's aide edging around the pole with the dangling IV bottle. She set a tray on the table by my bed. "Sit up now," she said with a coaxing smile. "See if you can eat something."

"If I'm sick enough to be in the hospital, why don't they let me sleep?" I grumbled. But I raised my bed, and she rolled the table in front of me.

"How do you feel?" Mom asked me as the aide hurried off on her next errand.

I eyed the eggs, like smears of Elmer's glue across my plate. "I don't feel hungry, that's for sure. Where's Dad?"

"He went downstairs to buy a newspaper. You'd better eat that while it's still hot. In a little while they're taking you down the hall for the bone marrow test."

I set down my fork and pushed the table away.

"How do they do it? Dr. Echevarria never did tell me. Mom — it sounds awful!"

"We're allowed to be there with you," Mom said. "They numb it somehow. You won't feel anything."

Suddenly Elizabeth slid the curtain aside. "It's not so bad if you don't look," she advised. "Just don't let them show you the needle."

Maybe she was trying to help me feel better. But instantly I pictured the needle she said I shouldn't look at. The ones they used for drawing blood were bad enough. Now they were talking about sticking something right into my bone. It sounded like a scene from a horror movie.

"You were just kidding, right? When you said last night you've had *ten* bone marrow tests?" I asked.

Elizabeth shook her bald head. "Ten, maybe twelve. I don't remember. I get them every couple of weeks."

If she had had hair, Elizabeth would have looked almost normal — as normal as anyone *can* look sitting up in bed in one of those ugly hospital gowns. Even though her face had that strange, swollen look, I had the feeling that she must have been pretty not long ago. I wondered what was wrong with her. Whatever it was, I wouldn't let it happen to me. It was mind over matter, as Aunt Cynthia said.

I reached up and touched my hair for reassurance. It felt knotty and rumpled, but it was definitely still there. "The bone marrow test — does it hurt?" I asked.

"It's not like you'd think," Elizabeth said. "It's kind of weird, but it doesn't hurt except when they give you the local."

"What's a local?" I asked apprehensively.

Elizabeth's eyes widened, as if I'd said I didn't know what a plate was, or a glass of water. "The local anesthetic," she said patiently. "It's the stuff that numbs the place they take the marrow out of. Are you getting hip or breastbone?"

She sounded like Dad at the dinner table, passing out white meat and drumsticks. Only she was talking about my body.

I turned to Mom. "Do I *have* to have this?" I asked, choking back a sob. "Can't we just go home?"

"I wish we could," Mom said. She leaned over and gave me a long, warm hug.

That was all I needed to get the tears going. "I hate being here!" I cried. "Why is this happening to me?"

I heard a faint rattle as Mom closed the curtain. Elizabeth was going to think I was a real jerk, carrying on like this. I clenched my fists tight and drew a deep breath, fighting to get myself under control.

When I looked up, Dad stood in the doorway,

a folded paper under his arm. Dad always started the day with the newspaper. That much hadn't changed, even here.

Hastily I wiped my eyes on the sleeve of my gown. Maybe Dad wouldn't notice I'd been crying.

"Hey! Breakfast!" he greeted me. "That looks better than the so-called oatmeal I just grabbed in the cafeteria." He turned to Mom. "I ran into Barbara — you know, that nice nurse from London. She says they're just about ready, so maybe you ought to wait and eat afterward."

Suddenly a nurse arrived, pushing an empty wheelchair. "Want a free ride?" she asked. She wasn't offering me a choice. She didn't call me "love," either. She was tall and broad-shouldered and as American as a Big Mac.

"I can walk," I insisted. "I don't need that thing."

The nurse slipped my feet into paper slippers before they touched the floor. "We don't want to wear you out," she said. "Come on, hop aboard. This is the Treatment Room Express."

"There's nothing wrong with my legs," I protested. But I was too weak to resist when she slid her arm around my waist and eased me into the chair.

Mom and Dad forged ahead, clearing the way for my safe passage. If I hadn't been so scared it would have been a rather pleasant way to travel. With no effort at all, warm in my nest of cushions,

I cruised past all the people standing on ordinary legs — a little boy with a remote-controlled car, two girls looking at a bulletin board, a cluster of nurses laughing over some private joke. I coasted by a sunny playroom where a bunch of kids were building an enormous Lego castle, and out through the Pediatric Oncology doors. Then the nurse turned, guided me down a narrow hallway, and brought me to a stop.

The fun was over.

Big Mac came around on my left, and Barbara closed in on the other side. "Good morning," she said briskly. "You remember me, don't you?"

"Yeah," I said. "From yesterday."

"Perhaps you'd rather not, is that it?" Barbara asked cheerfully. "Perhaps you'd rather we met under different circumstances."

I nodded, too scared for small talk. "Let me tell you what we're about to do this morning," Barbara continued. "This procedure is called a bone marrow aspiration. Bones are hollow, and marrow is the substance inside them. It's a bit like a factory, the marrow is. It manufactures about ninety-eight percent of the blood that — "

"You don't have to explain it," I interrupted. "Just get it over with, okay?"

Barbara laughed. "It'll only take but a minute, love," she assured me. "Now, we need to look at your bone marrow in the laboratory in order to

out into the hall. Behind us, Dad asked, "When do we get the final results on all this?"

"The lab'll work it up today," Big Mac said. "It takes a while. The doctor should give you the rundown tomorrow morning."

All the way down the hall, I couldn't stop talking. "I felt like that needle made a hole all the way through me," I said. "If they ever told me I'd have to have bone marrows every couple weeks, like Elizabeth does — I wouldn't do it, that's all. I'd just say 'No way! Forget it! I'm outta here!' "

Mom and Dad let me talk. They couldn't have stopped me if they'd wanted to. I guess it was just relief that the ordeal was over.

"No way!" I repeated as they wheeled me back into room 708. "I don't care what happens, I'll never go through that again!"

# 7

As soon as I got settled back in bed, a strange nurse came in with another needle and a new bottle to hang from my pole. "This is a transfusion for you," she explained, attaching the new tube to the one already flowing into my hand. "Some fresh healthy blood will help you feel better."

"She's not kidding," Elizabeth said from her side of the room. "Whenever I get a transfusion I feel like going out and building a pyramid or something."

"I hope you're right," I sighed. "All I ever want to do anymore is sleep."

That afternoon, whenever I was awake, Elizabeth and I talked about school and our friends, about my swim team and her flute lessons. She had a lot of company. A grandmother, several aunts and uncles, as well as her mother and stepfather and her father and stepmother passed through in a muddled parade all day. Elizabeth introduced me and showed me the things her visitors brought her. She had a big cardboard box on the floor by her bed, overflowing with comics and paperbacks, puzzles and cassettes, and drawing supplies. A huge stuffed lion perched at the foot of her bed, and from the ceiling hung a balloon that read: *GET WELL SOON!*

I really liked Elizabeth when she acted like a normal person. But whenever the subject turned to sickness and the hospital, she became someone else. Her voice got deep and serious, as though she were a grown-up and I was only a little kid. She sounded almost proud when she told me she had leukemia, as though it were a badge of honor. I wanted to ask her how it had happened, what brought her to Memorial in the first place. I wanted to show myself that her story was utterly different from mine, that we had nothing in common. But I didn't ask. There were too many things I didn't want to hear.

No matter how hard I tried to change the subject, Elizabeth wanted to hand out advice. "Chemotherapy is tough, especially the first round," she told me that night, after the aide carted away our supper trays. "You can't even *think* about food without puking. Just keep your mind blank as much as you can, that's how I get through." Later, when a nurse stuck me three times before she found the vein she was after, Elizabeth remarked, "I don't let students work on me anymore. If they miss the first time, I make them get somebody who knows what they're doing."

"Elizabeth," I blurted out, catching myself by surprise, "what happened to your hair?"

"Oh, that." She touched the top of her head and giggled. "It's the chemo — you know, the drugs they give you in here."

"What do you mean?"

"These medications. They make your hair fall out."

"That's awful!" I gasped. "How can you stand it?"

"Oh, it grows back," Elizabeth said. "It takes a couple months. When I get out of here, I'll get a wig."

"You act like you don't even mind," I said, almost accusingly. That big-sister voice of hers was getting to me.

"Of course I mind!" she said. "But what's the use? I'd rather be bald than dead, I'll tell you that."

"I don't know how you stand it, being in here so much," I exclaimed. "I guess I'm lucky — I'll probably be home in another day or two."

"I thought the same thing at first," Elizabeth said in that infuriating, superior tone of hers. "I couldn't believe it, when they said I had leukemia."

"I bet they tell that to a lot of people who haven't even got it," I said. "When they get done with all their tests, they're probably going to admit I just have mono-whatever-it-is."

I glanced over at Dad, who sat in the chair by my bed, reading *Newsweek*. I waited for him to agree with me. He only turned the page and didn't say a word.

Just then Mom came back from the pay phone, where she'd been checking up on Crysti. "Aunt Cynthia says everything's fine," she reported. "You know, she thinks we ought to try some alternatives before we rush into anything. She says doctors push too many toxic chemicals."

"I notice she took Eric to an MD when he got hit with the baseball bat last spring," Dad said. "She just talks a lot of theories."

I wanted to ask what alternatives Aunt Cynthia meant, but I was getting tired again. Putting together the question, listening to the answer — all seemed like too much work. I made my magic bed go flat. That was the signal that I wanted rest, that I needed to be left alone.

I woke the next morning feeling the best I'd felt in weeks. It was as though I'd shed layers and layers of weariness, shaken off the fuzz that had clogged my brain for the past week, and burst forth strong and full of life again.

"You look like you feel a lot better," Mom said, beaming at me.

"I do," I said. "I feel like I could swim the hundred-meter."

"It's the transfusion doing its work," Barbara said, bending over me. She thrust a thermometer under my tongue. "Transfusions are wonderful!"

With the thermometer sticking out of my mouth like a lollipop, I could only shake my head and make faces. I had to wait for her to pull it out, sixty seconds later by her stopwatch, before I could exclaim, "Maybe the transfusion hasn't got anything to do with it. Maybe I'm just getting better."

"Here comes breakfast," Barbara said, as if she hadn't heard me.

"The biggest event in the day," I said, laughing. I hadn't realized until then how bored I was with hospital life. There was nothing to do but eat and get stuck with needles.

Now, for the first time in days, I had an appetite. I studied my tray eagerly, wondering where to begin. An apple lay on a saucer, smooth and round and irresistibly red. There was hot toast with marmalade, and a foamy glass of orange juice. Even the scrambled eggs looked edible.

"You're going to get a lecture from Dr. Etch this morning," Elizabeth commented. "He always gives you one after he gets bone marrow results. You'll get the special today, since it's your first time."

"It's my *last* time, too," I said, taking a crisp bite of toast. I decided to save the apple for later. It would be something to look forward to.

"Let's just wait and see what the doctor says," Mom cautioned. "If you need another test later on — "

"I won't," I told her, glowing with confidence. "I'm really starting to get better now."

After breakfast a sleek, sun-tanned lady named Mrs. Branford arrived. She looked as though she should be carrying a tennis racket instead of a clipboard, but she said that she was the social worker on the ward. She exchanged a few polite remarks with me, about what grade I was in and how I was feeling, and then asked to speak with Mom and Dad. In private. Maybe, they all said almost in unison, I'd like to take a little walk in the corridor.

I was feeling so great that I didn't even get angry. I did think of listening in again, the way I had at Dr. Lewis's office. But Big Mac was on the prowl, and she cleared her throat suspiciously when she saw me hovering outside the door. I had to let them discuss me and hope for the best.

As I set off down the hall, I almost forgot the conference going on back in my room. Despite the IV pole that I wheeled beside me like some grotesque extra limb, it was glorious to be up, clear-headed, and steady on my feet. I could feel my muscles stretching back into shape after the long days of immobility.

At the end of the hall, next door to the little kids' playroom, was the lounge — a bright, carpeted room with hanging plants at the windows and seascapes on the walls. A girl my age and a boy a year or two older sat at a round table, engrossed in a game of Scrabble, while MTV pounded in the background. They both had pale, doughy complexions — and the boy was bald. The girl had hair, but when she turned her head it shifted, and I realized that she wore a blonde wig.

"Hi," the girl said as I edged my way back toward the door. "You're new, right?"

"Yeah," I said. "I came the day before yesterday."

"My name's Jessica," the girl said, digging into the box of Scrabble tiles. "Don't mind Vince over here — he's a weirdo."

"Takes one to know one," Vince said cheerfully. "So what's *your* name, new kid?"

"Jill Marino."

"You coming to Group this afternoon, Jill Marino?" Vince wanted to know.

"What's Group?" I asked.

"It's for all the older kids on the floor," Jessica explained. "Outpatients, too. Anybody who wants to come. You talk about what's happening with you, and how you feel, and — you know, everything about having cancer."

"I don't have to go to that," I said. "They made me come in to have tests and stuff, but now I'm better."

Vince looked at me, long and hard, before he

spoke. "You know what Pediatric Oncology means in English? It means kids' cancer. They don't stick you on Pediatric Oncology for nothing."

"I'll see you guys later," I said. As I tried to escape, my IV pole jammed on a chair leg and I had to bend over and work it loose. Then it wedged against the door frame and forced me to stop again. For a frantic moment, I felt as though the lounge had hold of me and would never let me go. Then at last I broke free and fled back to my room, the pole gliding smoothly at my side.

Dr. Echevarria overtook me as I reached the door. "Well," he said, "nice to see you up and around. You're just the young lady I'm after."

Behind his big round glasses he looked like a friendly owl. It was hard not to smile back at him, but I managed. I didn't want to be found. I wanted to get away where none of them would be able to talk to me again.

"Are your parents in there?" he asked. "I need to talk to the three of you together."

"They're in there," I said.

Mrs. Branford and her clipboard were gone. Mom sat with her empty hands in her lap. Dad stood by the window, gazing out at the parking lot. They both turned as Dr. Echevarria ushered me in.

"I think it would be a good idea for us all to sit down and discuss Jill's test results," the doctor began. He trailed off, peering around at the bed, the nightstand, and the single straight chair. "Well," he amended, "I guess we *can't* all sit down in here, can we? Just make yourselves comfortable wherever you can; this won't take too long."

I climbed up onto the bed. Dad and Dr. Echevarria stayed on their feet, facing each other with the room between them.

"The results are in on the bone marrow we drew yesterday," Dr. Echevarria stated. "I'm afraid the test is positive."

Dr. Etch, I thought. That's what Elizabeth called him for short. Dr. Etch.

"There are a lot of leukemic cells," Dr. Etch went on relentlessly. "The tests confirm what your pediatrician suspected. Jill has ALL — acute lymphocytic leukemia."

An icy finger slid down my back. The chill spread all through me. I hunched against the pillows and pulled the blankets up over my knees.

"Mrs. Branford explained it," Dad said. His voice was flat. "She just left."

"Well, I may be able to answer a few of your questions," Dr. Etch said. He paused, but none of us had any questions to ask. "It's a lot to take in," he said. "Believe me — if you have to have leukemia, ALL is the best kind to get. There are several types of leukemia, you know — about twelve in all. Right now ALL has the most favorable prognosis of any of them. I mean by that, we can predict the most hopeful future. We get

74

long-term remissions in about sixty percent of the cases."

"What about the African cockroach?" Somehow my own voice amazed me. It sounded exactly as it always had.

"The what?" Dr. Etch stared at me, bewildered.

"You know — the new medicine. The cure made of the juice from this big ugly bug. It was in the paper."

Dr. Etch shook his head. "I'm not sure I know what you're referring to," he said. "Right now there isn't any definite cure. Still, a lot of patients get into a remission that lasts and lasts, and they go on with their lives. I saw a boy just yesterday — he's a sophomore at Ohio State. He's been in complete remission now since he was fourteen."

"I'm thirteen," I said. "What about me? What's going to happen to me?"

"Let me explain first just what leukemia is. The name comes from ancient Greek words that mean 'white blood.' That's because it's a disease in which the body makes too many white blood cells — cells that never fully mature to do the work they're supposed to do."

I shook my head. None of it made any sense. But Dr. Etch went on talking. "That's why leukemia is a form of cancer. In cancer, you see the wild growth of certain abnormal cells — they grow out of control. That's what happens in leukemia. These abnormal white blood cells — think of them as the bad guys — they start crowding out the healthy cells — the good guys. It gets harder and harder for the blood to do its job — to carry oxygen to all the body's tissues, to fight off infections, to mend wounds."

"What's going to *happen?*" I repeated. "I thought I was better! I thought I could go home!"

"Well, not quite yet," Dr. Etch said. "First we have to get you into remission. That means we've got to get rid of the bad guys, so the good guys can take over again."

"Mrs. Branford talked about a course of chemotherapy," Dad said in the same strange, flat voice. "What will that be, exactly?"

"We'll be using some very powerful drugs," Dr. Etch said. "Mostly methotrexate. We give them intravenously, right into the veins, to get them straight to the bloodstream. They kill the abnormal cells, the ones that are growing so fast. If everything goes properly, we'll have her out of here in one to two weeks."

"And then I'll be okay?" I asked eagerly. "I can get back to normal and everything?"

"Yes — for the most part," Dr. Etch said. "When you're in remission, you'll have no restrictions as far as school, recreation, anything like that. But you *will* be on medication for the next three to five years. You'll have to come back into the hospital from time to time, for drugs that we can only give while you're here, and for regular spinal taps and bone marrows so we can check your progress."

*Bone marrows.* He said it so casually, condemning me to that monstrous needle, that unbelievable stabbing pain. . . .

"You need to understand that these are very powerful drugs," Dr. Etch said. "When they go after the leukemic cells — the bad guys — they may attack some normal ones, too. You see, we don't have drugs yet that are smart enough to know the difference."

All the while we talked, I hadn't seen Mom move. Now she spoke up for the first time. "You mean side effects?" she said. "That's what you're saying, isn't it?"

"Side effects can be — unpleasant," Dr. Etch said. "But they vary from one person to another."

"Am I going to lose my hair?" I asked frantically.

"It doesn't happen to everyone," Dr. Etch said. "Let's just deal with side effects as they come, all right? Maybe we'll get lucky."

How could he talk about luck? I wondered. If I had any luck at all, I'd be at the Y, swimming laps. I'd be sitting in Amanda's kitchen, listening to a story. Or fighting with Crysti over which TV channel to put on. I wouldn't be trapped here, behind those double doors marked PEDIATRIC ONCOLOGY.

# 8

"It's not fair!" I moaned. "I felt so good yesterday, and now they ruined it!"

Mom put a fresh, cool washcloth on my forehead. Her face was blurred behind a white gauze mask. "Just think about getting better," she said. "Going home in a week or two."

"That means for the next week or two I'll be stuck in here, feeling like this."

Elizabeth wasn't kidding when she said chemotherapy was tough. Waves of nausea swept over me whenever I moved. My head pounded, and my mouth had erupted in canker sores.

I was never alone. Mom and Dad hovered over me constantly, and nurses were always in and out. But they were all well people. Their bodies had never turned against them, the way mine was betraying me. They could never understand how scared and angry and miserable I felt.

Being sick separated me from everyone around

me. I had never imagined that I could be so lonely. And to make matters even worse, they had moved me to an isolation room. "It's not that anybody's going to catch leukemia from you," Big Mac had assured me as she wheeled me down the hall a few minutes after Dr. Etch's lecture. "Leukemia's not contagious like chickenpox or the flu. But these drugs you're going to start, they can really lower your resistance. We don't want you picking up any germs you won't be able to fight off."

Now I lay in a tiny closet of a room, my bed draped with sterile curtains. The doctors and nurses, Mom and Dad, all had to wear masks when they came in. Danger hung in the air outside my tent — deadly germs clamoring to get in and carry me away. I would receive methotrexate for 24 hours, and then remain on antibiotics until my immune system had a chance to revive. For my own protection, the nurses said, until this round of chemotherapy was complete, I must stay in isolation.

Elizabeth said she survived chemo by making her mind a blank. But I couldn't stop the thoughts from coming. Between bouts of vomiting, strange, tangled ideas wound their way through my mind. I thought about those people called untouchables in India. I'd read about them once — the lowest of the lowly, people kept apart from all the rest of society. I was like one of the untouchables, I decided. A barrier of gauze masks and rubber gloves stood between me and all the normal people who came and went so freely.

If I could tear down my tent and burst outdoors, if I could fill my lungs with a fresh breeze and feel grass under my bare feet, maybe then the leukemia would go away. No one could get better like this, tormented by medication that seemed to make me sicker, shut away from the real world, in isolation.

The next afternoon, Dad came and stood beside my bed. "I'm going to pick up your sister and take her home," he explained. "She's been at Aunt Cynthia's for three days now. She needs to get back to a normal routine as much as she can."

"What about me?" I cried, seized with panic. "You're not just going to leave me here by myself!"

"Of course not," Dad said soothingly.

"I'll be here with you," Mom added, "and later if I go home, Dad will come back."

"But Dad — couldn't you just stay a little longer?" I asked. "Just till they let me out of this cubicle? They say it'll only be a couple more days."

Dad shook his head. "Your mother and I talked it over while you were sleeping," he said. "At this point, you don't need both of us here at once. And your aunt Cynthia says Crysti's started having nightmares. She must be feeling sort of forgotten."

I knew he wasn't abandoning me. Mom would still be here. But I didn't like the idea that Dad was going away. It would make my isolation even more complete. "Wait till tomorrow, at least," I begged. "Just one more night."

"I'll be back tomorrow afternoon," he promised. "I'll call tonight and find out how you are."

I don't know why I started to cry. This was really so unimportant, just a tiny sliver of the big awful thing that had happened to me. But I began crying, long and loud. Here in isolation, there was no Elizabeth to shame me into acting my age. I cried and cried and didn't even try to stop.

Finally, through my own desperate sobs, I heard Dad saying my name. "Jill!" he called, almost shouting to reach me. "Jill, all right. If it means that much to you — I'll stay here one more night. I won't go until tomorrow morning."

The crying had me in its clutches. Even when I wanted to stop, the sobs still shook me, one after another. But very slowly my body began to relax. One of the nurses, who must have rushed in during the commotion, helped me blow my nose and wiped my face with a cloth smelling of disinfectant. "All right now," Mom said. "Don't worry. Tonight we'll both be here with you."

The nurse hooked another bottle into my IV tube. I think it was some sort of sleep concoction, because in a few minutes I felt myself beginning to drift.

True to his word, Dad stayed at the hospital that night. He camped out on a couch in the lounge, and Mom slept on a folding cot in my room. They were both there with me when I woke up retching in the middle of the night, and through all my misery I felt them trying to help in every way they knew how.

When Barbara arrived in the morning, she threw me her most bracing smile. "Feeling better?" she asked. "It won't be long now. You've met methotrexate and you've lived to tell the tale. No mean feat, I should say."

"And I've still got my hair," I said, sweeping it back from my face. "I guess I got lucky in one thing at least. But that medicine is awful stuff!"

Naturally Barbara jumped to the defense of chemotherapy, just as I knew she would. "Methotrexate is our frontal attack, you might say. It does away with a good number of those nasty white cells."

"It almost did away with *me*," I told her. "I didn't know it was possible to feel so sick."

"It's a rotten business," she sighed. "But you can say good-bye to methotrexate for now."

"Good-bye and good riddance!" I said, with more energy than I knew I had. "I hope I never go through that again."

Barbara busied herself with my bottles and IV lines. She didn't make any promises. "Now we've called in the reinforcements,"she said, like a general drawing up a battle plan.

"What do you mean, reinforcements?" I asked. Mom and Dad both leaned in close, taking in every word.

"The reinforcements," Barbara said briskly, "are medicines to build up your healthy cells. The ones we want to see grow and prosper."

"The good guys," I said.

"Do these new drugs have the same side effects?" Dad asked. "She started on them yesterday afternoon, and she had a rough night last night."

"The antibiotics are much more easygoing," Barbara assured us. "But the methotrexate will stay in her system for a while yet. She'll feel better little by little."

"When can I get out of isolation?" I demanded.

"Four or five more days," Barbara said. She paused to write something on the chart posted at the foot of my bed. "And Jill, as soon as we see you're in remission, you can leave us. I guess that will just break your heart now, won't it, love?"

"Once I get out of here," I declared, "I'm never coming back!"

The thought of home filled me with a deep, yearning ache. Nothing on earth could be so sweet as my own room. In all my life I had never truly appreciated its blessings — peace, privacy, the chance to surround myself with my special, favorite things. Perhaps I could dare to believe the things Barbara was telling me. Perhaps the worst was over, and I would really be home again soon.

With my hopes fluttering back to life, it wasn't so hard to say good-bye to Dad that morning. By the time he left, I felt well enough to sit up. I even worked a crossword puzzle on a tray across my knees. I was about to give up on the bottom right-hand corner when a nurse's aide came in and handed me a fat square envelope. Instantly I recognized the wild, sprawling handwriting. It was a letter from Amanda.

Hungrily I tore the envelope open.

*Dear Jill,*

*I was taking out the trash this morning when Mr. Marlewski yelled over to me that you were in the hospital. I tried to call you a couple of times and nobody ever answered, so I thought maybe you went away somewhere. But he said your mom called him because you were all at the hospital, and he had to take in your mail. He told me what's wrong with you, but my mom says he's an alarmist. Remember that time he called the cops because he heard somebody prowling around in his backyard, and it was just Bobby Sherman out there looking for his baseball that went over the fence? My mom says not to take him too seriously and just wait till we hear from your folks. Right now all kinds of crazy rumors are going around. So what really is the matter? When will you get home???*

*This Saturday we're going up to Kelley's Island fishing. Dad won't let us eat fish from the lake because the pollution causes cancer. But he still likes to catch them, even though he just throws them back. Fishing is boring, but I like to walk around up there. You can climb on the rocks and it's really pretty.*

*I just learned to make these paper swans off a video my mom got, so I sent you one. It's Japanese origami. If you unfold it carefully you can figure out how to do it.*

*Do they let you make phone calls from there? (Gee, it almost sounds like you're in jail. But you even get one free call from jail, don't you?) Call me up or write to me or send a pigeon with a message! Just let me know what's really happening to you! You're my best friend and I want to know.*

*Love,*
*Amanda*

I shook the envelope, and a white paper swan floated onto my tray. For half an hour I lost myself in its mystery, until I mastered the art of making paper swans of my own.

I read Amanda's letter over and over, but I didn't try to call her. That night, as the nurses were changing shifts, I got Mom to bring me some writing paper and tried to compose an answer. "Dear Amanda," I began. "Mr. Marlewski isn't an alarmist this time. It's true. I really am sick. I have leukemia. Maybe I got it eating fish from Lake Erie . . . "

I read back what I had written. The words stared up at me, bold and cruel. *I have leukemia.* In big black letters it seemed somehow more real than anything Dr. Etch had said aloud. I have leukemia, I thought. Maybe I'm going to die.

I crumpled the page into a ball and dropped it into the wastebasket by my bed. Dad must have seen Amanda now that he and Crysti were home. He could explain everything. I would take the cowardly way out.

After that, the get-well cards flooded in. I got one from the Marlewskis, and one from the Shermans. I had a card from Katie Rosario, and one from Sue, and a big fancy one from Mrs. Brownlow that everyone on the swim team had signed, even Larry. There was a whole stack of cards from kids I knew at school, and a note from Mrs. Rush, last year's English teacher. It gave me a warm, happy feeling, to know that so many people were thinking about me and sending good wishes. But it made me sad in a way, too. I didn't want to be in the hospital, looking at pretty cards with cats and butterflies. I wanted to be home, face-to-face with the people who were my friends.

Mom and Dad took turns staying with me, just as they said they would. On Tuesday I finally got out of isolation. They put me back in my old room, 708. Elizabeth had left, and we had the place to ourselves.

When Mom arrived on Wednesday morning she announced that she had a surprise. In walked Crysti, waving the strangest bouquet I had ever seen. It bristled with leafy twigs and pinecones, and in the middle were three huge sunflowers.

"Wow!" I exclaimed. "Where'd that come from?"

"We stripped the gardens bare," Crysti said, grinning. "Me and Bobby and Linda Sue and Amanda. We picked every flower we could get our hands on."

"The neighbors must have loved that," Dad said, shaking his head. "The way the Marlewskis pamper their garden . . . "

"People were really nice," Crysti protested. "As soon as they knew it was for Jill they let us take anything we wanted."

I buried my face among the petals and drew a long breath. Some of the daisies were already wilting, and dry twigs tickled my nose. But this was the closest I could get to a deep, healing lungful of fresh breeze.

"Thank you," I said fervently. "Thank everybody from me, okay?"

I held the bouquet at arm's length to get a good long look at it, all those little bits of home. Suddenly something moved, a black speck among the sunflower petals. I looked more closely, and spotted another speck, and another. They marched from the heart of the great yellow flower in a long, winding procession. The bouquet was alive with tiny black ants.

"Eew!" I cried, thrusting it back into Crysti's hands. "It's got bugs in it!"

She stared at me, appalled, as I brushed frantically at my hands and face. Something was crawling down inside my nightgown. Something darted across my pillow. I shook my sheet, and a shower of ants tumbled to the floor.

One of the aides helped me change into a fresh gown. She shook out the blankets, put clean sheets on the bed, and carried the flowers away. All the while, Crysti kept moaning, "I'm sorry! I'm sorry! I didn't know!"

"It's okay," I tried to assure her. "It's even funny, when you think about it."

Nobody was laughing. "Yeah, right," Crysti said. "It's the funniest disaster I ever caused!"

"I should have thought of it myself," Mom said wearily. "I should have checked the flowers before we brought them in."

"Don't everybody get so bummed out!" I protested. "It's not a disaster! It's just something that happened. A diversion! We can use some diversion around here." There I was, propped up in bed with drugs dripping into my veins, trying to console the rest of the family. Well, I thought, maybe it wasn't any stranger than the rest of the things that had happened to me over the past few days.

Crysti looked as if she was ready to cry. "I just want everything to go back to normal!" she wailed. "I don't like all this." She swept her hand in an arc that included room 708, Pediatric Oncology, and all of Memorial Hospital. "I want this to be over so we can go back to the way we're supposed to be."

"That makes two of us," I said fervently. "It's one thing the two of us can really agree on!"

# 9

On Monday afternoon, twelve days after I entered the hospital, I finally went home. As farewell presents I handed out paper swans to all the nurses, reserving the two prettiest ones for Barbara and Big Mac. No matter how much I argued and complained, they had been good to me. I knew I owed them a lot.

It was lovely to be vertical, looking straight out at the world instead of staring up at spots on the ceiling. It was wonderful to walk down the corridor on my own, free from the IV pole with its swaying bottles. I still felt a bit unsteady, probably from spending so much time lying in bed. But my bruises were gone, and, according to Dr. Echevarria, my blood count was just what it should be. I was definitely on my way back to normal.

"You're in a good remission," Dr. Etch explained that last morning. "But that isn't the same as a cure. There are still leukemic cells hiding out, waiting to attack later on. That's why you need to stay on medication, and I want to see you at my office every two weeks."

That wouldn't be so bad, I told myself. I could put up with the long drive each way, and the probing and the needles, as long as I could stay out of the hospital.

"And," Dr. Etch said, breaking into my thoughts, "in six or eight weeks, we'll want to bring her back in for another bone marrow. She'll need some more IV medication, too. Just a precautionary — "

"Not another *bone* marrow!" I exclaimed. "I'm not going through that again!"

"It's not for a long time," Mom consoled me. "Don't even think about it yet."

"I hate bone marrows," I said flatly. "I told you before, I'm not going through that again."

"You know, treatment for leukemia is pretty rough," Dr. Etch told me. "With kids your age, we find it works best to keep them informed, and let them handle as much responsibility as they can. When you get home, do you think you can keep track of your own medication?"

"Sure," I said. "What's the big deal about that?"

"Well, it's more complicated than you might think. We'll give you a chart showing which medicines you have to take on which days."

"I can read a chart," I said. "Don't worry." I'd promise anything, I told myself, if I could only get out of here.

"That's what I like to hear," Dr. Etch said. "And coming back into the hospital every so often is another part of your treatment. It's not much fun, but it's part of the program to get you well."

"It's the part I can do without," I said, with a feeble laugh.

Dr. Etch let the matter drop. "Well, I know you folks are anxious to be on the road," he said. "I won't keep you. But any questions you have, anything that seems the least bit out of the ordinary — don't hesitate to call."

Mom thanked him, shaking his hand as they said good-bye. Dr. Etch turned to me. "You can get back to all your regular activities," he assured me. "When does school start?"

"Next Wednesday."

"Great. You're just in time. You won't have to fall behind."

"Can I go back to swimming?" I asked. "I'm on a swim team."

"You bet!" he said. "Exercise is terrific for you. Don't let anybody treat you like an invalid."

"I won't," I said. "I don't want them to."

"You might want to come to our weekly support group," Dr. Etch said. "It meets right here at the hospital. It's a chance to talk to other people who are going through the same things you are. You feel like you're not so alone."

"Forget it," I said brusquely. "It's bad enough having this. I don't want to sit around with a bunch of other sick people *talking* about it!"

"A lot of kids find it very helpful," he insisted. "You ought to give it some thought."

I shook my head. "I'm okay on my own," I said. "I just want to get back to the way things were."

"Well, you're doing nicely," he said, smiling from under his owl spectacles. "Keep up the good work."

I wanted to tell him that *I* wasn't doing anything. I came into the hospital sick; they filled me with drugs that made me even sicker; and now that they had stopped giving them to me, I was recovering at last. *I* had nothing to do with any of it. I was as helpless as a Ping-Pong ball, swatted back and forth between paddles.

But I wouldn't let my helplessness drag me down. I was going home. Oh blessed, glorious, wonderful Home!

Oberlin was waking up from its summer sleep. A notice in the window of the clothing store on Main Street announced BACK TO SCHOOL SALE, 15 PERCENT OFF. I spotted a flock of college kids hovering in front of the Co-op Bookstore. It was a sign that the season had changed, like seeing the first robins in spring. The last of summer had slipped by without me.

The welcoming committee burst onto the porch the moment we drove up — Dad and Crysti and Amanda and the Sherman kids, shouting and waving and pointing to their masterpiece. It flapped from the limb of the maple tree in the front yard — an old white bedsheet, adorned with swirls and flourishes of blue and green and yellow paint. In the middle, in proud red letters six inches high, they had written: JILL WE LOVE YOU.

Tears burned my eyes. I had such a wonderful family, such good, generous friends! Even Crysti, my pesty little sister, had forgotten our years of civil war. She had really missed me — and, I admitted to myself, I'd missed her, too.

"Mom — did you know about this?" I asked, dabbing a tear from my cheek.

"They've been working on it all week," Mom said, laughing. "Amanda's mother let them do it on her kitchen table."

As we climbed out of the car they swarmed down the steps, all talking at once. Before I reached the porch, Mr. and Mrs. Marlewski were waving over the fence. Mrs. Williams called a greeting from across the street, a pair of toddlers wrestling at her feet.

"You look terrific!" Mrs. Marlewski said. "You just need a little sun now, to bring back your color."

"Jill, you want some lemonade?" Crysti asked. "We made some — in case you're thirsty or anything."

"Are you allowed to have sweets?" Amanda wanted to know. "My mom was afraid maybe you weren't supposed to eat certain things."

"I can eat anything except hospital food!" I exclaimed as we trooped inside. In the middle of the dining room table stood a magnificent layer cake that shouted WELCOME HOME in pink icing.

Crysti poured me a cup of lemonade and insisted on handing me the first slice of cake. I still didn't have much appetite, but it looked a lot better than any food I'd seen in the past twelve days.

Somehow I felt inspired to make a speech. "Hey, you guys," I said, gazing around at their grinning, eager faces, "you really do make me feel great. I mean it — you're the best thing that's happened in weeks!"

"Who did all the cleaning?" Mom asked suddenly. "The house was a wreck when I left yesterday."

Dad patted Crysti's shoulder. "This kid's been working like a demon. You should have seen her! First thing this morning she was running around with the Pledge."

The house really did look nice. The furniture sparkled, the kitchen floor shone, and the usual heap of newspapers by the back door had magically disappeared.

"Well, Crysti, I'm impressed!" Mom said, giving her a hug. "You've been a big help through all this, you really have."

Crysti beamed, and I felt an unaccountable twinge of envy. In the old days, you couldn't get

Crysti to hang up her jacket or straighten her room. She was always tossing wadded-up socks into corners, and dropping candy wrappers on the carpet. Now all of a sudden she was a big help. And I was only a problem, a constant worry, the cause of all the upheaval in the house.

I wasn't being fair, I tried to tell myself. If Crysti had gotten sick, I would have scrubbed and dusted and made banners. She would have been the source of anxiety while I was the hero of the day.

Anyway, I wouldn't be the pampered invalid for long. "This cake looks delicious," I said and took the first heavenly bite.

After everyone had eaten and the neighbors said good-bye, Mom reminded me that I ought to take it easy. This was my first day home from the hospital, after all. I knew dimly that I was tired, but I was too excited to slow down yet. "I've had enough naps for a lifetime," I said and led Amanda up to my room so we could talk in peace.

My room was just as I had left it, except that someone had made the bed. My posters covered the walls. My silver cup for last year's swim championship still stood on the dresser, between my jewelry box and my ceramic piggybank from Mexico. The afternoon sun spilled through the curtains, making familiar patterns on the rug.

"So," I said, flopping onto the bed, "what's been going on around here?"

Amanda looked up at me from a cushion on the floor. "Not that much," she said. "It's been pretty quiet."

"Did Megan get home from camp?" I asked. "I bet she's got some good stories!"

"I saw her Sunday," Amanda said. "Yeah, she said she had fun."

I tried again. "Have you seen anybody else? Who's been hanging around?"

"Oh, I don't know." Amanda studied her nails. "Mostly all anybody really talked about was — " her voice dropped, "was you."

"Well, I'm here." I managed a laugh. "I don't look like a ghost, do I?"

"Not a ghost, exactly — but you're pretty pale," Amanda said. "You don't look like you used to."

"So what do they say, when they all talk about me?" I wasn't laughing anymore. It was hard to keep a tinge of annoyance out of my voice.

"Nobody can believe it. People just keep saying to each other, 'It's not really true. You don't think it's *true*, do you?' "

"Like when Teddy Donovan got killed in that car accident?" I asked.

Amanda nodded. "Like that," she said and looked down at her nails again.

I would never forget the morning we heard about Teddy. It was two years ago, when Amanda and I were in sixth grade. We walked onto the playground at school, and no one was running around or kicking a ball. People just stood in little clusters, talking or staring into space. And Iris Block, who always loved to tell bad news, came up to us with a look of doom on her face and said, "You don't know, do you? . . . Teddy Donovan died last night."

Teddy was in seventh grade, a year ahead of me, and I really didn't know him very well. But his face haunted me for weeks after he died. I kept picturing him with his disheveled blond hair, and his Cleveland Browns jacket, and his tennis shoes that always looked as if someone had stepped on his heels. I remembered the time he sat next to me in assembly, drawing pictures of monsters in his notebook. I remembered the day we got out early because a pipe burst in the basement, and Teddy leaped down the front steps yelling, "Jailbreak! Jailbreak!" Each time those memories crashed in on me, I jolted once more against the terrible, impossible word, *dead*. Teddy Donovan, one of us, just an ordinary kid with an ordinary life. Finished. Forever. Dead.

I sat up so suddenly that I felt dizzy. "Amanda," I said, "you can tell them I'm *not* Teddy Donovan! Tell everybody that you've seen me, and *I'm alive!*"

# 10

"Tomorrow's Labor Day," Crysti remarked over supper Sunday night.

I stared at my plate, trying to call back my long-lost appetite. Dad reached for the butter. No one said a word.

"Labor Day," Crysti repeated. "The first Monday in September."

Slowly I absorbed her message. Labor Day was special in our family. Every year for as long as I could remember, we marked the close of summer with a trip out to Cedar Point, the big amusement park at Sandusky. It was a glorious day of sun and thrills, hot dogs and cotton candy and dizzying rides, before the reality of school set in.

"Yes," Mom said, "I guess you're right."

"Well?" Crysti asked. "Are we going?"

Mom and Dad exchanged a meaningful glance across the table. "I don't really think — " Dad began.

"Why not?" Crysti demanded. "Please? We al-

*ways* go to Cedar Point! I've been looking forward to it all summer!"

"Oh, Crysti," Mom sighed. "We hate to disappoint you. But really, the way things have been going . . . "

Crysti turned to me. "*You* want to go, don't you, Jill? *You* can talk them into it."

I gnawed a few kernels from my corn on the cob. I thought of bumper cars, whirligigs, roller coasters . . . My stomach churned rebelliously. "I don't know," I said. "I don't really feel like it. Not tomorrow."

"It's just too much this year," Dad said. "We've got so many other things to deal with — we'll just have to skip Cedar Point for once."

"It's not fair," Crysti muttered. She glared sullenly at her plate. "We never have any fun anymore."

"As soon as they reopen in the spring, we'll go," Dad promised. "Memorial Day, how about that?"

"Sure," Crysti said, but she sounded as if she didn't believe him.

It hadn't taken long for the welcome-home glitter to wear off, I reflected. There was a tension in the atmosphere which I had never noticed in the old days — the days before I went to the hospital. Mom and Dad walked around as if they couldn't remember how to smile. Mom was so tired she'd taken a week off from work. Sometimes Dad would stare at a book in his hand for fifteen minutes without turning a page. The two of them worried over me day and night. Sometimes I let them fuss, too tired and discouraged to resist. At other times, I snapped at them to leave me in peace. Meanwhile, Crysti was forever tugging Mom's arm, bursting in on my quiet times, whining for attention. We were all pushing and pulling, and toppling in a dozen directions at once.

People we barely knew kept calling to ask how I was — professors from the college, real-estate clients of Mom's, even old Mrs. Angerhauser, who'd moved to Ashtabula. Each day the mailman brought a fresh stack of get-well cards. I knew it was good of people to think of me, to care so much. But all the cards, the calls, the worried glances, and the anxious questions made sure I never forgot that I was ill.

I was the center of this flood of attention and concern. Crysti was almost invisible, wandering through the house, hovering at the edges of conversations, sitting alone on the stairs. For an incredulous moment I wondered if she might actually be jealous of me. Well, I was the one who ought to be jealous! Crysti was free from pills and needles and dire statistics. A random fate had made her healthy and given me leukemia.

On Wednesday morning, Dad dropped me off at school. I clambered out of the car, my backpack bulging with brand-new pencils, pens, and spiral notebooks, my eyes searching out familiar faces. I waved to Iris Block, who stood with a group of girls at the edge of the schoolyard. For a moment she just stared at me, wide-eyed and disbelieving. Then she turned to the others, and they drew together, whispering and pointing at me over their shoulders.

As I approached them, I found myself walking more and more slowly. At last I drew to a stop and looked at them from a few feet away. "Hi," I said. "What's going on?"

"Hi, Jill!" Iris cried. "How *are* you?" She came down heavily on the question, as though she wanted the full details.

"I'm fine," I told her. "How was your summer?"

Iris hung on to her subject like a dog playing tug-of-war with a rubber bone. "We all heard about you getting sick," she said. "We didn't know if you were coming back to school or not."

"Well, it looks like I'm here," I said. "Hey, my mother says she heard they hired a new science teacher. Mr. Plummer — isn't that a weird name?"

"Yeah, right," said Iris. She was still staring at me, as though I'd grown an extra hand. I looked past her to the others — Lori Armstrong and Megan McMurray. "This guy Plummer, he's supposed to be real young," I said. "Like this is his first year teaching, I think."

Lori looked blank, but to my relief Megan ventured a smile. "Neat!" she said. "We can all break him in."

"Remember when we had that substitute last year," I began, "and John Tilman organized everybody to drop their books all at the same time? She was totally freaked out! Remember?"

Lori finally cracked a grin, and Megan giggled. But Iris hadn't dropped her bone. "I was so worried when you were in the hospital," she said. "A lot of people thought you might — you know — people thought you might — "

"Well, I didn't. Come on, can't we talk about something else?"

"Oh sure," said Iris, all apologies. "I'm sorry. I guess you *wouldn't* want to be talking about it all the time. I mean, if *I* had — a disease like that — *I* probably wouldn't want to talk about it, either. It's just that everybody was thinking about you a lot. We only want to know how you are."

"I know," I said. Maybe I was being mean, unappreciative. "It was really nice getting your cards," I added, speaking to all three of them together. "Thanks a lot."

Lori spoke up for the first time. "Is it really true?" she asked, her voice so low I had to bend forward to hear her. "Is it true that you have — leukemia?"

I jumped back a step, as if she had smacked me. I still couldn't hear that word without flinching. "It's not like you think," I said. "You get better these days. The doctor says I can do everything. I'm back to normal — completely."

"That's great," Lori said. "I always thought — leukemia — " She left the sentence dangling, unfinished.

"I didn't know they had a cure," said Iris. She almost sounded disappointed. She wanted melodrama, I thought, a chance to shed tears over a real-life tragedy.

I backed further away, scanning the schoolyard for an escape. Suddenly a car door slammed, and Amanda sprinted toward me. "Jill!" she cried. "Hey, I like your outfit!"

Without a backward glance I left the others to join her. "Wow!" I gasped. "You just saved me from Iris Blockhead!"

Amanda smiled knowingly. "Old Gloom and Doom," she said. "She told me once she loves sad movies that make her cry."

"*I'm* not a movie," I said.

The bell rang, and we ran for the door. I pelted up the steps, swept along by the laughing, shouting crowd. For eight years now I had experienced this first-day rush of excitement — the thrill of greeting old friends, the curiosity about new teachers, the dread of a fresh regimen of tests and homework. Today was just one more first day, like all the others. I was one more eighth-grader, ready for a glorious, privileged year at the top of the heap.

But this year I was different. I wasn't just Jill Marino, B student, competitive swimmer. I was the kid who'd been in the hospital. The girl with leukemia.

All that day, and through the days and weeks that came after it, I sorted my classmates and teachers into two categories. There were The Ones Who Knew, and The Ones Who Didn't Know.

The Teachers Who Didn't Know got annoyed if my homework was late and didn't listen to excuses. When they caught me passing a note to Amanda, or trying to sneak out of assembly five minutes early, they threatened me with a detention — and I could tell they meant it. The Kids Who Didn't Know were mostly sixth- and seventh-graders, people who barely remembered my name. I recognized them by the way they never gave me a second glance. Intent on their own business, they marched past me in the halls as if I were part of the decor.

The Teachers Who Knew, on the other hand, tended to be very impressed by my assignments, even if my handwriting was sloppy and I dashed the work off in the morning before breakfast. If they scolded me at all, they looked uneasy, even pained. I could almost hear their thoughts as they watched me: *Poor Jill! This may be her last year on earth!* How could they force me to write "I will not talk during class" 100 times?

Luckily, not all of The Kids Who Knew were like Iris Block. Most of them never mentioned the hospital or leukemia to me out loud. But sometimes in the cafeteria, or out on the school lawn, they fell silent as I approached, and I sensed that they'd been talking about me. Once when I had an extra-big load of books to carry, Megan McMurray rushed to help, as though she thought I was too frail to manage on my own. Another time, Lori Armstrong invited Amanda to a slumber party but didn't ask me. Amanda tried to soothe my hurt feelings. "It wasn't Lori's fault," she explained. "Her mother said no. She said if you got sick or something, she didn't want to be responsible."

In the beginning, The Kids Who Knew were only my old friends. But by the end of the first week of school, the whole eighth grade belonged to the club. And after I had a bad reaction to one of my medications and missed three days of school, all of my teachers knew, too.

As Dad put it, you had to be a rocket scientist to keep track of my medication schedule. Every morning I had to swallow an anticancer pill called, for some reason I never understood, 6-MP. Every night I choked down a nasty-tasting little white prednisone tablet. Morning and night on Mondays, Wednesdays, and Fridays, I got Septra, an enormous, pink antibiotic. And every Thursday I had to take six tiny, viciously powerful methotrexate pills. I had a handy supply of thorazine tablets, which were supposed to help if I felt nauseous from the methotrexate. At the end of the first four weeks, I began a whole new schedule, with a new set of drugs and instructions.

The doses were lower than when they had me in the hospital, but I still had what Dr. Echevarria called "a few unpleasant side effects." Sometimes my mouth broke out in horrible canker sores. Sometimes my joints ached as though I were an old lady with rheumatism. And there were days when I couldn't keep food down, when I curled up on the couch under the afghan and wondered what I had ever done to deserve so much misery.

I ran into a stretch like that at the end of September, when Dr. Etch switched me to some new pills. Through a long Wednesday, Thursday, and Friday I stayed out of school, too sick to care who found out what was wrong with me. Mom brought home my assignments, but I didn't even glance at them until Friday afternoon. I did two pages of math and then pushed my books aside. Endless months of treatment loomed before me, round after round — uncounted days of torture. What was the use of working for good grades? What was the use of anything?

I clicked on the TV and flipped through the channels, searching for something to pull my mind away from my troubles. I bounced past *Jeopardy* and a couple of talk shows and discovered an afternoon movie. A boy and girl walked hand in hand across a college campus, its stately old buildings thick with ivy. Peaceful and lovely, the scene was exactly what I longed for. It reached out and drew me in.

Soon I was engrossed in the story of Jenny and Oliver, who were so much in love. Oliver's rich father didn't want them to get married, because Jenny was Italian and her father ran a bakery. But the couple went off to a justice of the peace, and it looked as though they would live happily ever after. . . .

During the next set of commercials I thumbed through the TV listings in the paper, wondering what else might be on. To my surprise I found that the movie I was watching, *Love Story* starring Ali McGraw, wouldn't be over for another hour. Jenny and Oliver couldn't live happily ever after quite yet. Some complication was about to enter their lives.

At last the commercials were over. I tucked the afghan around my feet and waited to see what would happen next.

What happened was that Jenny got sick. The doctor told Oliver that she had leukemia.

I couldn't believe it. I wanted to escape, to rewind back to that green campus and those two carefree kids with life spread out in front of them. But the movie rolled forward, and I couldn't tear myself away.

Slowly, gracefully, Jenny was dying. She faded like a flower, folding and drooping until at last she lay in her hospital bed, ready to breathe her last. All the time Oliver hovered beside her, loving, grieving, unflinchingly devoted.

I couldn't stand it any longer. I grabbed the channel changer and clicked the two of them into oblivion. But I couldn't shake free of their story. It was the sort of movie Iris Block loved — a "three-hanky special." But it didn't make me cry; it only made me angry. Jenny never had canker sores or ugly bruises. She never gagged and moaned over the toilet bowl. She was brave and beautiful to the very end.

Crysti peered around the door frame. "Can I put something on now?" she asked. "I want to see this rerun of — "

"No!" I growled. "I'm watching a movie."

"You are not. You turned it off."

"Well, I'm going to turn it on again," I said, punching the clicker. Jenny's hospital room flashed onto the screen once more.

Crysti came in and flopped into a chair, draping her legs over the armrest. "What's this about?" she asked.

"Did I say you could watch it?"

"Well, you don't own the TV, do you?" she snapped. "The living room isn't your personal kingdom!"

"I can't watch with you in here blabbing!" I exclaimed. "Just get out of here, will you?"

Crysti sat up straight, but she didn't leave. "What's the matter?" she demanded. "What are you getting so mad for?"

"Cause you keep bugging me, that's why!" It wasn't Crysti's fault that I was angry and sick and miserable. But I felt like screaming at somebody, and she was the handiest target. "Go on!" I told her. "Just leave me alone, all right?"

"You're really mean, you know that!" Crysti's voice shook with tears. "I'm telling Mom!"

"Go ahead. See if I care." I had a right to be mean, didn't I? They couldn't expect me to go around smiling courageously like Jenny in the movie.

"Mom!" Crysti yelled. "Jill's picking on me again!"

"What do you mean, *again?*" I flared. "I've been lying here all afternoon, minding my own business!"

"What about this morning," she shot back, "when I wanted to borrow your tank top?"

"You've got plenty of tank tops! You don't have to borrow my stuff all the time!"

"Mom!" she called again. "Make her quit it!"

Mom hurried in and stood between us. "Please,"

110

she begged, "please will you stop this fighting!"

"All I did was — " Crysti began.

But I interrupted her. "I just want to have some peace," I pleaded. "She's always bothering me!"

"Crysti," Mom said with decision, "come help me in the kitchen. Let Jill rest for a while, okay?"

"Okay," Crysti said sullenly. "I'm going." She stalked out of the room without a backward glance.

I felt like the queen in *Alice in Wonderland*. I could say anything I wanted, and no one dared to oppose me. People would rush to obey if I shouted, "Off with her head!"

I turned up the volume on the TV and settled among the sofa pillows. My peace and quiet were guaranteed.

I didn't really want to watch the end of *Love Story*. I didn't want to sit there and watch Jenny draw her final heroic breath.

I clicked off the set again and sat in the sudden, ringing silence. There was nothing to do, no one to talk to. I had all the solitude I could ask for. And suddenly I ached with a deep and bitter loneliness. Nobody, no one in the world, could ever understand.

# 11

"**H**op in!" Mom called from the car window. "Look who's here!"

Aunt Cynthia waved to me from the passenger seat in front. She'd been dropping by once or twice a week lately, ever since I got out of the hospital.

Crysti slid over as I scrambled into the backseat. "Hi," I said, to everybody in general. I stuffed my towel into the bag with my wet swimsuit.

"How was practice?" Mom asked, pulling out into traffic.

"Not too bad." I didn't feel like discussing it. In two weeks we had a big meet with Mansfield. I'd counted on entering, doing my best for our team as I always did before. But this afternoon Mrs. Brownlow announced that I would be an alternate. I still might get to swim, she assured me. If someone had to drop out . . .

Of course she had to think of the team. She couldn't get hung up on not hurting my feelings.

I'd practiced hard, but I'd never caught up with myself after my summer slump. I wasn't a disgrace, exactly — but I wasn't indispensable, either.

The worst part of all was Larry. He'd never paid me a lot of special attention in the old days, but now he avoided me whenever he could. Sometimes I caught him staring at me, awed and a little afraid. He couldn't forget that I'd almost passed out in the water, that they'd hauled me out of the pool half-drowned. He never referred to that day aloud, but he didn't have confidence in me anymore. I felt that he was always waiting for me to do something unexpected and terrible again.

"How are you feeling these days?" Aunt Cynthia asked. "You've put on a little weight, your mother says."

"I'm okay." I tugged a comb through my damp, tangled hair.

Aunt Cynthia wouldn't settle for the easy answer. She wanted details. "I hear they just started you on some new drug. How's it going?"

"I guess it's not any worse than the other one."

"See what I mean?" She turned back to Mom as though I'd proved a point. "It worries me, you know? They're pumping her full of toxic chemicals. It's wild when you think about it — the idea of treating disease with all these poisons! You need to get the body back into balance."

"We're doing everything we can," Mom said. "She's eating plenty of grains, and fresh fruits and vegetables. And she gets lots of exercise, especially with her swimming. We know that's all important."

"That's terrific. You're headed in the right direction. But maybe you need to rethink some of the other stuff — you know, all the drugs."

I glanced at Crysti. She looked back at me and shrugged. We'd both heard a lot of this before. Whenever Aunt Cynthia stopped by, she and Mom talked long and hard, around and around. Usually they waited until I was out of the room, and I only caught enticing fragments of what they said. But today the argument was spilling into the open.

"The doctors — standard medicine — they've helped an awful lot of people," Mom insisted. "We have to take that into account. They've got the track record."

"I'm not pushing you or anything," Aunt Cynthia said. "Look, I brought Jill some green tea. It can do wonders."

"Thanks," Mom said. "We'll give it a try."

I leaned forward eagerly, resting my hands on the seatback in front of me. "Could I really just drink green tea," I asked, "and quit taking pills?"

"It's a little more complicated than that," Aunt Cynthia admitted. "But basically, yes, in this natural treatment program I read about, you'd get away from laboratory chemicals. You'd be taking only natural things into your body."

"Mom," I demanded, "can I? Can I at least try it?"

"I wish it was that simple," Mom said. "We can't just drop everything and go off on some wild goose chase. We've got to do what makes sense."

"It makes sense to quit taking all this junk that makes me sicker," I muttered.

"If you and Mike would just consider — " Aunt Cynthia began.

Mom cut her off. "Mike has enough on his mind right now," she said. "Don't worry him with this, all right?"

No one spoke for the next two miles. I gazed out at the fields of cornstalks sliding past the window.

We were turning into town when Crysti spoke up. "We're doing a skit at school," she announced. "For Columbus Day."

"That's nice," Mom said distractedly. "Are you in it?"

"I'm a Carib Indian," Crysti said. "They lure me on board the ship and take me back to Spain."

"You'll need a costume, won't you?" Mom sighed. "I'll find the time somewhere, I suppose."

"The costume's easy," Crysti assured her. "Can you and Dad see the show? It's a week from Friday, in assembly, at ten o'clock."

"Ten in the morning?" Mom asked. "Friday?

That's the day Jill goes to Cleveland to see the specialist."

"What specialist?" I demanded. "Nobody told *me* about this!"

"Dr. Echevarria just called this morning," Mom said. "There's a famous doctor coming in to give a lecture or something, and Dr. Echevarria picked a couple of his patients for this guy to see. Kind of a special consultation."

"Thrills," I grumbled. "I can't wait."

"So that means you're not coming," Crysti said.

Mom shook her head. "I'm really sorry. We can't make any changes. This doctor's only in town for two days."

"What about Dad?" Crysti asked. "Can *he* come?"

"I doubt it," Mom said. "He teaches two classes on Friday mornings!"

"So nobody's coming," Crysti said, kicking the back of the driver's seat. "I should have known!"

"I wish I could go," Aunt Cynthia offered. "Only I can't get off work. My boss'd kill me."

"Never mind," Crysti said with a noisy sigh. "I don't care. So what if I'm the only kid in the skit with *nobody* in the audience?"

"I told you I'm sorry," Mom exclaimed. "Now be reasonable! Just try, all right?"

A brooding silence settled over the car again as we drove down Main Street, until Mom parked in front of the drugstore. "I've got to run in for a refill on one of Jill's prescriptions," she said. She slammed the car door in time to miss Aunt Cynthia's disapproving sniff.

The second she was gone, I touched Aunt Cynthia's shoulder. "Talk them into it," I pleaded. "They've got to listen to you."

"It's up to your mom and dad," Aunt Cynthia said. She reached up and squeezed my hand. "Everybody wants what's best for you. You know that, don't you?"

"Yeah," I said. "I guess so."

Crysti stared out the window at a couple of college kids playing Frisbee on the square. She didn't say anything to either of us.

In a moment Mom was back, springing into the driver's seat again. A paper bag crinkled on her lap — a bag full of little plastic containers with childproof lids. Little containers of poisonous pills — for me.

"Your bloodwork is terrific," Dr. Echevarria informed me after the consultation with the famous specialist, Dr. Monroe. "You're handling the medications very well, and your platelet count is up to 200,000."

I'd learned a lot about blood since the afternoon when I listened outside Dr. Lewis's door. I knew there were red cells that carried oxygen, and white cells that fought infections. Platelets helped with healing; if my platelets were low, I'd develop bruises again, and maybe have sore gums and nosebleeds. A good platelet count was good news.

Mom and I exchanged smiles of relief. It was the middle of October, nearly two months after my stint in the hospital, and we'd received good news each time Dr. Echevarria examined me. Maybe all those toxic chemicals were helping, after all. Some day soon, I told myself, Dr. Etch would announce that I didn't have to come in anymore. No more slow drives up to Cleveland. No more needles, no more solemn pronouncements about the state of my bodily fluids. I would walk away cured, and wave leukemia good-bye.

"You're in a good strong remission," Dr. Etch went on. "Still, we want to keep close tabs on your progress. I'm going to put you in the hospital for a few days next week for a spinal tap. That's a test of the fluid in your spine, to make sure there aren't any bad guys getting into your central nervous system. And you'll have another bone marrow test."

I didn't move. I sat on the table, my feet dangling, and stared him down. "I'm not going back in the hospital," I declared. "I'm not having a bone marrow again."

"It's a very routine procedure," Dr. Etch said mildly. "It's not a lot of fun, I agree, but it's a necessary part of your treatment."

"I'm not going back in the hospital," I repeated.

Dr. Etch switched into lecture mode. "Most

blood cells are formed in the bone marrow. If your leukemia is coming back, we can catch it early by doing a bone marrow exam. Then we can zap the bad cells right away before they have a chance to do any harm."

"I'm fine," I said. "You just told me so yourself. I don't need any tests in the hospital."

"Jill," Mom said, with a note of pleading, "you have to cooperate. You've got to do what the doctor says."

"You don't believe me, do you?" I demanded. "I'm *not going to the hospital!*"

"We'll talk about it back home," said Mom. "It isn't until next week."

"How does Monday sound?" Dr. Etch asked. "We'll probably have her home by Friday."

"Whatever's convenient for you," Mom assured him. "Monday's fine."

"Monday is *not* fine," I told them. "Neither is Tuesday or Wednesday or any other day. I'm not going back there, so forget it!"

Mom ignored me. She acted as though she hadn't heard a word I said. "Monday," she repeated. "We'll be there."

For the rest of that week, I went to school and swim practice, took my medications obediently, and worked out my secret plans. Hospital beds were hard to come by. If I didn't show up on time, my bed could be claimed by someone else. They would have to reschedule my bone marrow exam. It could be delayed three days, maybe a week. If I lost my bed a second time, and a third, they would finally get the message.

Mom had promised — or threatened — that we would talk about my trip to the hospital. But she and Dad must have had one of their private conferences and decided to leave me alone. All weekend they carefully avoided the subject. There were no lectures on maturity and cooperation, no speeches about doing my share to help in my treatment. I began to feel more and more uneasy. It wasn't normal for them to be so still.

On Sunday afternoon I checked the calendar in the kitchen. Monday's date was circled in red, and beside it Mom had written, *JILL 10 AM*.

They hadn't forgotten. They were soothing me into submission, hoping I would go resignedly when the time came.

That night, as I headed upstairs to my room for bed, Mom glanced up from her real-estate magazine. "We'll have to set the alarm for six tomorrow," she said casually. "We need to be out of here by seven-thirty to get to Cleveland on time."

I didn't answer. Pretending I hadn't heard her, I tramped upstairs to my room.

Crysti was in the bathroom. I peered in through the half-open door, wondering how long I'd have to wait. Water gushed in the sink, and she held the toothpaste tube in one hand. But instead of brushing her teeth, she made faces at herself in the mirror.

"Crysti!" I protested. "Hurry up, will you?"

"In a minute," she said. "How do you like this? It's my crazy face." Her mouth twisted into a ghoulish grin.

"Lovely," I said. "Hurry up so I can use the bathroom."

"I'm hurrying," Crysti insisted. "Just look at this. This is terror." She squeezed her eyes tight and lowered her head, hiding her face in her hands.

"Is that what you did in the Columbus skit?" I asked. "Was that to scare the explorers or what?"

"Oh, come on! It's almost time for the haunted house," she reminded me. "Halloween is only two weeks away."

The haunted house was an annual family project. Every Halloween we decorated the basement with cobwebs, created secret doors and booby traps, and dressed up as ghosts and witches to give nightmares to all the kids in the neighborhood. Usually Aunt Cynthia and Uncle Howard came to help, and Carla and Eric pitched in, too.

Crysti was right. Halloween was two weeks away.

"Mom and Dad haven't said anything," I ventured. "Maybe we're not doing it this year."

"You mean, on account of your being sick?"

"I don't know. Maybe."

Crysti's mouth drooped, and her eyes lost their sparkle. "Yeah," she said. "It'd be too much trouble, wouldn't it?"

She didn't complain that it was unfair. She didn't even ask me to use my powers of persuasion. She just seemed to fold up with resignation as she dabbed toothpaste onto her brush.

My whole family was out of kilter tonight. Mom and Dad didn't lecture me when I was stubborn. Crysti bowed her head and took her disappointment in silence. Everyone was too quiet, too careful. It was as though a monster had moved in, a demon who would roar down upon us if we didn't walk on tiptoe. I thought I knew what the demon was. It was the disease that had crept into our lives and torn our world apart. The monster was leukemia.

# 12

"Jill? *Jill!*"

Slowly I swam upward, my body light and graceful as I cut through the water. Someone was calling me, but the nameless voice was muffled and far away. I must have dived very deep, to have such a long swim back to the top. . . .

"Jill, it's time to get up! Come on now!"

I burst through the surface, out into light and sound and air. I was in my own bed, and Mom was knocking at my door.

It was Monday. They wanted to take me to the hospital.

Play it cool, I reminded myself. Let them think you're going along with them.

"Coming!" I called. I swung my feet to the floor and padded to the closet. I picked out a pair of jeans and a striped T-shirt — the sort of outfit I might wear if I were going someplace not too special. The hospital didn't rate anything fancy — *if* I was going there, which I wasn't.

Downstairs, breakfast waited on the kitchen table. "I checked with Dr. Echevarria. It's okay if you take your medication a little earlier than usual," Mom explained. "The sooner we get on the road the better."

The front door slammed and Dad came in with the paper. "I'll be back here after my eleven-o'clock class," he told Mom. "Give me a call around twelve-thirty, let me know how things are going."

They were so maddeningly calm. It was all a matter of logistics — keeping to my schedule, planning phone calls, beating the traffic. No one was going to stick a needle into one of *Dad's* bones. *Mom* wasn't about to be trapped in a hospital bed, tied to an IV pole. How could they understand what I felt? We lived on separate planets.

"Take your pills, and pack your overnight bag," Mom said when I carried my dirty dishes to the sink.

"Okay," I said, still quiet, still submissive. I got my morning pills out of the cupboard and downed them with a glass of water. "When are we leaving?" I asked.

Mom glanced at the clock. "I'd say half an hour. That'll give us plenty of time."

Half an hour. I'd make sure they didn't suspect anything until the last possible moment. "I'll get my stuff ready," I said and marched back up to my room.

Crysti was awake now, rattling around in her

room as she got dressed. I sat on my bed, hands idle on my lap, and listened to her singing from across the hall. It sounded like one of the little songs she was always making up, something lonesome and sad. She repeated the same two lines over and over,

> *I hate to think you have to go,*
> *It's too soon to say good-bye . . .*

The song faded. Crysti appeared in my doorway, still wearing her nightgown. "I guess you won't be here when I get home from school, right?" she asked.

"Guess again," I said.

Crysti frowned. "I thought Mom said you had to go back in the hospital."

"Yeah, you heard her right."

"Well, then I guess I won't see you for a couple of days."

"You won't have to wait that long." What kind of game was I playing with myself? There was no room for Crysti in my plans. She had the biggest mouth in the state of Ohio.

But I couldn't make myself stop talking. I'd been scheming for so long, I couldn't keep it to myself for another minute. Maybe by dropping hints out loud I was daring myself to go through with my plan, now that the time had come.

"They're not going to make you stay there?" Crysti asked.

"They're not going to make me do anything," I said. A wild rush of confidence streamed through me. It was true — nobody could do anything to me against my will. I was on my own, in charge of myself.

"Crysti! Are you ready for school?" Mom shouted from the foot of the stairs.

"Almost," Crysti said. She sidled out of the room, throwing me one last, puzzled glance.

"Are you about set, Jill?" Mom asked. Now she was just below me, on the landing.

"I still have to use the bathroom," I said. "I'll be down in a minute."

I shut the bathroom door behind me as Mom appeared in the hall. I heard her scolding Crysti for dawdling, warning her that she would miss the school bus if she didn't hurry.

If Mom looked into my room, she might wonder where I'd put my overnight bag. She wouldn't think to search for it under the bed. There it lay, empty and flat, going nowhere.

"Five minutes, Jill," Mom said firmly. "Be down on the front porch."

I leaned against the wall, listening to her feet descend the stairs. Then I opened the door a crack and peered out. Crysti was out of sight, banging drawers as she rummaged for clothes. I stepped into the hall and drew the bathroom door shut behind me, hoping to leave the impression that I was still inside. Then, on tiptoe, I crossed my room, slipped through the closet, and ran lightly up the narrow, twisting stairs to the attic.

At the top I hesitated for a moment. Mom and Dad would be furious. I couldn't imagine what they would do when they finally caught me. But no punishment they could dream of could ever be as bad as a return trip to Pediatric Oncology.

The attic door creaked as I pushed it open and crept into the musty dimness. From far below floated the murmur of voices, calm and unsuspecting. Then I drew the door softly closed, and a blanket of silence folded around me.

Streaks of morning light filtered through a dusty window, showing me a landscape of cartons and forgotten furniture. Stacks of boxes leaned precariously against the low, sloping ceiling. A wooden table lay like a stranded beetle with its legs in the air. I recognized the big gray steamer trunk that hunched in the corner; when I was little, Mom used to open it up and let me play with the old hats and dresses inside.

The haunted house we set up in the basement each Halloween was full of thrills and laughing surprises. But if our house harbored any real ghosts, the attic was their domain. Anything might lurk in its shadowy corners. A phantom from the past might feel quite at home among its sad, sagging chairs and boxes of crumbling relics.

I remembered Dad's stories about our house once being a station on the Underground Railroad. He said runaway slaves had hidden here for weeks at a time. I wasn't the first fugitive to crouch at the top of the house, nestled under the roof.

"Jill!" Mom's voice drifted up to me from another world. "Come *on!*"

I didn't answer. Every minute that ticked away was one more point in my favor. Let them call and wonder and search. If enough time slipped away, it would be too late for the trip to Cleveland.

Below I heard someone knocking on the bathroom door. My trick had worked; Mom thought I was still in there. "Jill! Are you all right?" she called, and I heard the door crash open.

"Crysti, have you seen your sister?" Mom's voice was high with annoyance and concern. I pressed my ear to the door, but I couldn't catch Crysti's answer. Then their steps clattered down into the distance, and my name filtered up to me as they called through the living room, the kitchen, and the den.

They thought I had gone downstairs, that somewhere I waited to climb meekly into the car. It hadn't occurred to them that I would escape.

The voices faded, then swelled nearer again. Dad's deep, commanding tones carried straight to the attic door. "Jill! This is no time for games! Get down here this instant!"

It was Dad's "or else" voice, warning of dire consequences. That voice didn't speak — it commanded.

I fought down the impulse to fling open the door and shout, "I'm up here!" But I couldn't think about Dad and Mom right now, I could only think of Memorial Hospital and that monstrous needle drilling into my bones.

Scattered words found their way through the floorboards. Mom: " . . . looked there already . . . no, no . . . " and Dad: " . . . try the basement again . . . "

Again I caught Mom's voice. "Crysti, did she say anything to you?"

"She said something funny about not staying overnight," Crysti began. "Something about — "

"About what?" Dad cut in. "Not staying overnight where?"

"At the hospital. She said something about that."

I clenched my fists at my sides. I couldn't trust Crysti with anything! When I got my hands on her, I'd kill her. . . .

"She could have slipped out the back door," Mom said, "while I was waiting in front."

"Call Amanda's house!" Crysti suggested. "I bet she went to Amanda's."

I heard them all hurry off downstairs again, and for a long while I was alone. A cloud of dust enveloped me as I settled into a wicker rocking chair. I stifled a cough and thought of Peter Rabbit, sneezing in the toolshed when he was hiding from Mr. McGregor.

I should have thought to wear my watch. It was hard to know how long I had been in the attic, waiting for the morning to slide by. When should I emerge and face the catastrophe that was brewing downstairs? What could I tell them, anyway? Mom had taken the day off to drive me into Cleveland. Dad might be late for his class if he spent the morning searching for me. They were trying to help me, and I was putting them through turmoil.

I was glad for the sunlight that found its way into the attic. It would really be scary up here at night. Even in daylight — what little there was — I could almost see a vague, looming shape back behind that old bureau. . . .

Maybe I ought to come out now. I'd explain how much I hated the hospital. Maybe I could make them understand. I'd persuade them to let me quit taking medication and try the treatment Aunt Cynthia talked about. I'd drink green tea and eat nothing but spinach and soybeans for the rest of my life, if only I didn't have to have another bone marrow test, another IV drip!

Somewhere downstairs a door slammed. Footsteps drew nearer, and Crysti's voice reached me. "What about the attic? She always likes to go up there."

For a moment I froze, too stunned to think. They were coming back, clumping up to the second-floor hall again. Then, without a pause, heavy steps thudded into the closet and up the last flight to the attic door.

I sprang from the rocking chair and scrambled behind a stack of boxes. I curled into a ball, tucking in my hands and feet like a turtle crawling into its shell. If I didn't twitch a muscle, if I didn't even breathe, perhaps they would go away again!

The door creaked open, flooding the attic with light and noise. "Jill!" Mom called from below. "If you're up here, come out!"

Dad's big brown shoes advanced a few steps, then stopped. "I don't see her," he began. "Unless — " Suddenly he strode forward. The stack of cartons shifted, slid aside, and I lay exposed and helpless.

Dad seized my shoulders and lifted me to my feet. "What do you think you're doing?" he demanded. "We were worried sick!"

"I'm not going," I said, but my voice sounded thin. "I told you I won't go."

"I don't believe this!" Dad exclaimed, steering me toward the door. "I can't believe you'd pull a stunt like this at your age!"

His voice shook, and his hands felt rough and

angry. I began to cry. "You don't know what it's like!" I sobbed as he herded me down the stairs. "You wouldn't want to go there either!"

Mom and Crysti met us in the hall outside my bedroom. "Thank God," Mom sighed. "I was afraid — I thought maybe — thank God you're all right!"

"You *were* in the attic!" Crysti exclaimed. "I *thought* maybe that's where you went."

"Thanks a lot," I said, scowling at her. "You really think you're smart!"

"I just — " she began.

"You just had to open your mouth, didn't you!" I shouted. "You couldn't just mind your own business!"

"Girls, please!" Mom broke in. "This is no time to fight."

I turned to her imploringly. If she and Dad were ever going to understand me, I had to reach them now. They had to realize how I felt! "Please don't make me go!" I begged. "It's terrible at the hospital! You don't know how bad it is! Please, *please* don't take me back there!"

"Jill." Mom stood in front of me and looked me straight in the face. "I wish I could say, 'Sure, just stay home, don't worry about your treatment,' " she said, and tears glistened in her eyes. "I wish that more than anything in the world! But I can't! Jill, we're talking about your life!"

"Please!" I repeated. "Please, can't I just wait till tomorrow?"

"You're going *now*," Dad said. "I don't want to hear any more arguments, Jill. Get into the car."

"But my overnight case!" I tried one last time. "I didn't pack!"

"Then you'll go without your slippers," Dad said. "You're going to be late. I'll call Admitting and tell them you're on your way."

I had no choice, with Mom in front of me and Dad behind. "All right," I said. "I'm going."

Crysti trailed after us to the car, silent and staring. Suddenly I felt ashamed of myself. I was the older sister. I was supposed to be the mature, responsible one. Now Crysti had seen me crying and begging like a baby.

Somehow my shame twisted into anger — anger at Crysti herself. "This is all your fault!" I told her. "You're on *their* side, aren't you! Why are you always such a goody-goody?"

"Jill, that's enough," Dad said. It had been a long time since I'd seen him get mad at me, but I'd finally pushed him over the edge this morning. In a strange way, it was comforting to hear the old bite back in his voice.

Mom climbed into the driver's seat, and I clambered in beside her. "Call me when you get there," Dad said from the curb. "Leave a message if I'm in class."

Mom nodded. "We'll manage," she said. "It'll be okay."

She turned the key in the ignition, and the house receded behind us. Through the rearview mirror I saw Dad and Crysti watching from the lawn. Dad waved, strong and decisive, as though the gesture of his hand could speed us on our way. Beside him Crysti seemed small and fragile. I felt sorry for the words I had thrown at her, but it was too late to tell her now. The words of her song echoed through my mind, "Too soon to say good-bye."

# 13

"**D**o you remember me? I'm Mrs. Branford. I'm the social worker on this floor."

Slowly I turned my head on the pillow. The familiar parade had marched through my room for two days now — nurses and aides checking my IV lines and taking my temperature, doctors asking questions, volunteers offering puzzles and books and good cheer. Mrs. Branford was one more face, thrusting itself into the narrow territory above my bed.

"Hi," I said. I closed my eyes and hoped she would get the message.

"Could we talk for a minute?" Mrs. Branford asked. Noisily she worked loose the chair that was wedged under my tray-table. Whether I wanted to talk or not, she was here to stay.

"Sure," I said. "What else is there to do?"

I opened my eyes again and took a better look at her. I recognized her now, though her summer tan had faded. She was still tall and athletic, with a short, no-nonsense hairdo.

I glanced around for Mom, but she must have stepped outside while I dozed. Mrs. Branford and I were on our own. "What do you want to talk about?" I asked.

"Well, as a social worker, it's my job to kind of come in and help out any time there's a problem." She stopped, giving me a chance to comment. My head hurt, my stomach rolled menacingly, but I was alert enough to catch the key word. *Problem.* My story was out.

The silence stretched out, from strained to painful to downright impolite. At last I had to say something. "They must keep you busy up here."

"How do you mean?"

"With so many sick kids. Being sick — that's about the worst problem there is."

"Sometimes being sick is just a piece of it," Mrs. Branford said. "It's bad enough — but other things can make it even worse. Those are the things I can try to help with."

"I bet my mother told you all about what happened yesterday, right?" I said.

"Not *all* about it," Mrs. Branford said. "I won't know *all* about it till I hear *your* side."

I had to admit that was a good answer. I pushed the magic button and raised my bed so I could sit up. "I didn't want to come back here," I said. "I made up my mind not to. So — " my voice dropped. "So I hid in the attic."

I had felt so shrewd at the time, taking control of my own life. But now, explaining it aloud, the whole idea seemed hopelessly childish. I didn't want to discuss it with Mrs. Branford. I wanted to erase the whole memory.

"Nobody likes to come in here," Mrs. Branford said, nodding. "It's not exactly a day at the beach."

"But I'm stuck here," I said. I lifted my left hand, the one with the needle taped in place, and gestured toward the forest of IV bottles hanging over the foot of my bed. "My aunt Cynthia says they're poisons, all those medicines. That's why they make me throw up so much."

"Anticancer drugs *are* toxic," Mrs. Branford said. "So are antibiotics, as a matter of fact. It's their job to kill the bad guys."

"Yeah, I know," I said. "Dr. Echevarria told me all about it."

"The treatment we put you through is rough," Mrs. Branford said. "But right now it's the best we can offer you. It's the only thing we know of that works."

"Right," I said. "They *all* tell me that — Dr. Etch, and Barbara, and Big Mac, everybody."

"Who?"

"I mean that nurse named Shirley," I said. "I just call her Big Mac in my head."

"Big Mac," Mrs. Branford repeated. "Have you got a nickname for me?"

"How about Tracy?" I said. "You know, after Tracy Austin. Because you always look like you ought to be playing tennis."

"Sounds good to me," she said. "How about it? Do you play?"

"No, I swim. And at school I was in cross-country last year." I stopped. I hadn't expected to talk so much. I almost felt that we were making friends.

Mrs. Branford glanced at the empty bed across the room. "No roommate yet this visit?" she asked.

"No. I'm here by myself."

"It must get lonely now and then," she suggested. "I bet you wish you had somebody to talk to."

I remembered Elizabeth, with her advice and warnings and her round bald head. "Not really," I said. "Most of the time I feel too crummy to talk."

"But being sick is kind of a lonesome business," Mrs. Branford forged ahead. "Sometimes it helps to share how you're feeling with somebody else who's going through it, too."

"What for?" I demanded. "I want to think about other things besides leukemia. I just want to get out of here and have a normal life again."

"Every kid who comes in here wants that," Mrs.

Branford said. She leaned forward, resting one lean, strong hand on the bedrail. "We have a group of kids that gets together once a week," she said. "A support group, it's called. They can talk about anything they want — how they deal with procedures like spinal taps and bone marrow tests, and what helps when you're on chemo, and how to answer the questions kids ask at school, anything."

"I know about that group," I said. "Vince and Jessica told me."

"Well, they get together Friday afternoon. Why don't you sit in?"

"I don't think I want to," I said. "Thanks anyway."

"You could tell them all the names you call the staff," Mrs. Branford said hopefully. "They've got a few of their own, come to think of it."

"I don't want to go to any group," I said again. I kept my voice low and firm. I was in my own private place, the attic again, but this time it was a refuge in my own mind. Nobody was going to drag me out.

"Why not?" Mrs. Branford asked reasonably. "Can you explain it?"

My head throbbed. I wanted to lie down. But I had to tell her something, to make her understand. "A lot of those kids — Elizabeth and Jessica and that boy Vince — they act like they're right at home here," I began. "They act like there's

139

nothing to it. They don't even mind losing their hair."

"Well, that's good, don't you think? To be able to accept what's happening to you. That way it's easier to live with it, wouldn't you say?"

"I don't *want* to live with it!" I exclaimed. "I don't *want* to get used to it! I don't want to have leukemia, period."

"Of course you don't. Of course," Mrs. Branford stood up and tried to pat my shoulder, but I twisted away from her hand.

"I just want to wake up some morning and find out this was all a bad nightmare!" I told her as the first tears came. "That's all I want! And talking doesn't help! Nothing ever helps, ever! Nothing at all!"

I went home on Friday. Dr. Echevarria said my bone marrow was very good — four percent, whatever that meant — and I was free for another six weeks. Free, except for my ongoing regimen of pills.

"Oh, Jill! How *are* you!" Iris Block cried when I walked into school Monday morning. "What happened? Amanda said you had to go back into the hospital!"

"No," I said. "I was on a cruise."

Iris looked at me, not sure whether I was kidding. "Amanda said you had to have tests. What for?"

"For my scuba diving lessons," I said. "To find out how far down I could go."

"You're really brave, you know that?" Iris said in awe. "If I had — you know — if I was sick like you — I wouldn't be able to make jokes."

For a second or two I just stared at her in amazement. "I might be a lot of things," I said at last, "but *brave* sure isn't one of them."

Somehow, in spite of Iris, I slid back into the daily routine. There were book reports to write and maps to draw. John Tilman got suspended for cheating on a math test, and that gave everyone something new to talk about. I welcomed any distraction, anything to draw people's attention away from me and my illness.

"Are we going to have a haunted house this year?" Crysti asked one night at dinner. "Halloween's almost here."

"It's kind of late to put it together," Dad said after a pause. "I think maybe we'll have to take a pass on it this year."

"It figures," Crysti said, staring down at her plate. "No Cedar Point, no haunted house. . . . We never have any fun anymore."

She was right. Life at our house revolved around doctor's appointments and medication schedules. There never seemed to be room for anything else. "Why can't we do it?" I protested. "Is it just on account of me?"

"Don't feel like it's your fault," Mom said hastily. "I just don't think I've got the energy for it right now. It's gotten so elaborate the last few years — it's an awful lot of work."

"*We* could do the work," Crysti suggested. "Me and Jill. And Aunt Cynthia and all of them will help, like always."

Mom shook her head. "It's not just the decorating," she sighed. "It's having all the kids in the neighborhood tramping through the house. Up the stairs, down the stairs — it's too much."

"What if they didn't have to tramp through?" I asked, with the dawn of an idea. "What if we could let them right into the basement?"

"How?" Dad asked. "It's not like we've got a basement door to the outside, like some houses."

"Through a window," I said. "I've got an idea. We can make a slide. Got any old planks, Dad?"

In ten minutes it was all decided. Reluctantly at first, then with a spark of the old excitement, Dad agreed to help build a slide from the window ledge to the basement floor. Crysti and I would hang cobwebs, put up witches and black cats, and rig the basement with scary booby traps. By the time we were ready for dessert, even Mom had come around.

"But this is *it*," she promised. "The last year ever, unconditionally."

"Unconditionally," Crysti agreed. "This will be the last, and the best ever."

It was wonderful to throw ourselves into a proj-

ect, snatching wild ideas out of the air. I didn't
know how I thought of the slide, but suddenly it
was there, so real I could almost touch it, and we
were going to make it happen.

"I'll get some paper," I said, jumping up from
the table. "I want to make some drawings. We
could make a trap with blankets that fall down
when you walk under them."

I had reached the bottom of the stairs when
Mom's voice hauled me back, back to the reality
I lived in now. "Jill," she said, "don't forget your
medicine."

# 14

I went to the Y on Mondays and Thursdays to swim laps. I worked hard at the pool. I was determined to improve my time, to push myself back to the place where I'd been before I got sick. I didn't much care about winning races anymore. Mostly I wanted to show Larry and Sue and everybody else that there was nothing wrong with me, that I was as good as I'd ever been. But by the end of October, my effort still wasn't paying off. I never had as much energy as I needed. Sometimes my joints ached unbearably. One of the medicines I was taking — prednisone — made me gain weight. Also, "irritability" was one of its side effects. I was not amused when Crysti made up a song,

*Prednisone, prednisone,*
*Take it too much, you'll be living alone!*

"You're doing great," Larry said one afternoon as I climbed out of the pool.

I shivered inside my towel. "You think so?" I asked, with the first flicker of hope I'd had in weeks.

"I mean it," he said. "We all give you a lot of credit, sticking with it the way you do."

"Oh," I said. "It's no big deal. I'm all right." He wouldn't forget. Even if I turned into the best swimmer on the team, to Larry I would always be the girl with leukemia.

The clamor of the locker room couldn't shut out my thoughts. I wasn't really all right, and everybody knew it. My loose-fitting tank suit failed to conceal my body's sags and bulges. And my face stared back from the mirror, pallid and puffy. I looked like Elizabeth and all those other kids at the hospital. But at least I wasn't bald. Despite all the medication I'd taken, I still had my hair.

"Anything the matter?" Sue asked, coming up beside me. "You look kind of down."

"Just thinking," I said. "Not about anything very interesting."

I was spared more questions by a shriek from Katie Rosario. "Help!" she cried. "Help! Emergency!"

We both whirled around as she dashed from the bathroom, wrapped in a soggy blue towel. "There's no hot water!" she screeched. "It's *freezing!*"

145

"Great," Sue muttered. "Just what we need."

"I'm going to *die!*" Katie exclaimed. "I'm an ice cube! I'm a block of ice at the North Pole!"

"I'd better tell the guy at the desk," Sue said. "They'll have to call somebody."

"Yeah," said Katie, gathering her clothes from a bench. "Before we all die of frostbite."

Her words reached me from far away. My gaze was fastened on the comb in my hand. Its teeth were clotted with tangles of dark hair.

By now most of the other girls had straggled in from the pool. Everyone clustered around Sue and Katie, mourning the fact that there would be no hot showers this afternoon. No one noticed as I dropped the knotted clump of hair into the wastebasket. I ran my comb over my head — one stroke, two, three . . .

For a moment I closed my eyes. Until I saw it, I could hope that it wasn't true. But I had to look. I had to know for certain.

When I glanced at my comb again, there was no mistake. Heavy snarls of hair twisted among its teeth, and trailing wisps drifted away on currents of air.

My hand shook as I touched the top of my head. I half expected to feel a bare spot, but my fingers found nothing amiss. Still, the comb lay on my palm, shrouded with knotted strands.

The worst had begun. It was happening to me. My hair was falling out. . . .

I don't remember stuffing my wet things into my bag, or saying good-bye to Sue and the others in the locker room. Somehow I found my way to the parking lot, greeted Dad, and climbed into the backseat of the station wagon beside Crysti. For a while I managed to tune out her chatter. Her words rattled around my ears like hailstones, a lot of meaningless noise. But at last I realized she was talking to me, about the haunted house.

"What?" I asked. "Dad did what?"

"The *slide!*" she said, thumping the seat with impatience. "Weren't you listening? The slide is up!"

I pictured a stream of little kids swooping down the slide into the chamber of horrors we had designed. I'd be there to greet them, the Monster of the Basement, howling strange incantations, bald as an eggplant. . . .

I thought of Jessica, that girl in the lounge at the hospital last summer. Jessica wore a wig, but you could tell it wasn't her own hair. A wig could blow away in a high wind and leave you stranded, with total strangers gaping in amazement. Still, wearing a wig would be better than walking around the way Elizabeth did, with all that smooth pink scalp exposed.

A wig was a feeble solution. I'd never find one

to match my own hair, and everyone would know the truth. I could just hear Iris Block. "Oh, Jill!" she'd gush. "It looks gorgeous on you! Do you take it off when you sleep? Doesn't it itch? . . . "

"You've got to lean way back," Crysti said. "Otherwise you could clobber yourself on the top of the window frame."

For a moment my mind was blank. I couldn't imagine what she was talking about.

"Jill!" Crysti nudged me with a sharp bony elbow. "What's the matter? Aren't you even *interested?*"

"Sure," I said dully. "You've got to lean back. I heard you."

"I thought you wanted to do this!" she exclaimed. "We were working on it together, and I thought you were all excited."

I turned and stared out the window. "Right," I said. "I can't wait."

Crysti wasn't ready to give up. She leaned forward and tapped Dad's shoulder. "Did Mom buy cider?" she asked. "We always have apple cider and doughnuts in the kitchen, remember?"

"We'll have a regular assembly line going," Dad said a little grimly. "Down the chute, through the basement, up to the kitchen, chow, out!"

A wig was the only answer for kids who went bald. But the best solution was to hang onto your hair.

Prednisone made you grumpy and fat. Baldness was one of the blessings of drugs like vincristine, that they gave in the hospital. But I was home now; I hadn't had vincristine in days. Maybe one of the pills I took every day was to blame. I'd been lucky for almost three months, but they were catching up with me at last.

My medicines had turned against me.

"Don't forget your pills," Mom said automatically the next morning after breakafast.

"How *could* I forget?" I asked. "Jill Pill, that's my name." I carried my dishes to the sink and opened the cupboard where we kept all of my medications. I glanced at the chart taped to the inside of the door, listing my complex schedule. I rattled the bottles noisily, counting out the morning's dose aloud. "One Septra, one prednisone, and one six-MP."

The 6-MP, maybe that was the culprit. I clenched the pill in one fist and reached for a glass of water.

Mom barely looked in my direction. I knew which pills were marked on my chart, and she trusted me to swallow them all.

"What time is all the excitement supposed to start tonight?" she asked, pouring herself a cup of coffee.

"As soon as it gets dark," Crysti said. "Um,

Mom, I hope you got a *lot* of cider and doughnuts. I have a feeling we might have more kids than usual."

"How come?" Mom asked. She watched as I gulped my prednisone and my antibiotic. I hesitated, my heart racing.

"They canceled the party they usually have at the park," Crysti said. "Now everybody's talking about coming to our house."

"Bring them on!" Dad said from behind the newspaper. "We can handle it!"

"The more the merrier," I said. With one deft gesture, I dropped the 6-MP into the pocket of my jeans.

"I guess I'd better pick up some more provisions," Mom said. "I was just expecting the neighborhood kids. How many do we usually have — twenty, twenty-five?"

Crysti giggled. "Don't be too surprised," she said. "I think this year's going to be a little different."

No one had noticed. I was safe! I wouldn't let myself go bald!

But suppose something happened to me, I thought with a stab of fear. Without the anticancer pill to fight them, suppose the bad white blood cells began to take over? I remembered how sick I felt last summer before the hospital, so tired and weak I could hardly stand up.

But I was beyond that now. I was in a good

strong remission — Dr. Echevarria said so. I might look pudgy, but I felt almost normal.

I'd take my prednisone. I'd take my antibiotic. They could fight the bad guys for me. But I would never take 6-MP again. I wasn't going to lose my hair!

# 15

We ate an early supper that night, setting up a card table to make room for Aunt Cynthia's whole tribe. We were all in our haunted-house costumes, and the meal was a slapstick comedy. Aunt Cynthia kept making faces, practicing her witchy grimace, and every now and then Uncle Howard in his skeleton suit felt called on to let out a ghoulish groan. When Eric, in his flapping vampire cape, pointed to the catsup and uttered, "Please pass zee blood," Crysti and I almost fell onto the floor laughing.

We were cleaning up the kitchen when the doorbell began to ring. "They're here!" Crysti cried, bounding out to the front hall. "It's starting!"

Uncle Howard and Aunt Cynthia, Eric and Carla thundered down the basement stairs to get into position. I started for the door and hesitated, glancing guiltily back toward the cupboard. Even though I was skipping my 6-MP, I had other pills to swallow. But tonight, pills could wait. This was a special evening, too wonderfully normal to ruin with medicines.

"I'll be guarding the entrance," I called to Mom, who was busy getting doughnuts out of the pantry. She didn't stop me as I slipped outside. She didn't say a word about checking my chart.

The air was fresh and cool, scented with dry leaves and a tinge of wood smoke. I hurried to my place beside the open basement window. My ghost's sheet fluttered around me in the breeze. "Lean way back!" I warned in low, wavering tones as the first little girl threw her legs over the sill. "Watch your head! Low bridge!"

"Wheee!" she shrieked, zooming away out of sight. From within I heard a witch's cackle and one of Uncle Howard's very best moans. Chains rattled, and Carla's shivery voice called, "Come here, my little pretty! I won't harm you!"

A line was forming now. Linda Sue Sherman came next, dressed as a princess. She was followed by the two oldest Williams kids, dressed as Mickey and Minnie Mouse. Then came a crowd of girls from Crysti's class at school — I counted eight of them before I lost track. Mr. Marlewski arrived, with his red-haired grandson Ryan in a robot costume.

"Lean *way* back! Low bridge . . . " I wished I could turn on a recorded message. "Careful, don't bump your head."

"Haunted houses are a rip-off," Ryan stated. "They're all fake."

"I wouldn't be so sure," I said ominously and gave him an extra push.

By now a line of kids and parents stretched up the driveway to the street. As I watched, three cars pulled up, and a dozen more people piled out. Crysti wasn't kidding when she said we might have a bigger crowd than usual this year.

"Can you believe this?" Crysti asked, bouncing up beside me. "Mom's having a cow! Dad just ran out for more doughnuts, and a couple extra gallons of cider."

"I'm back!" announced Ryan the Robot. "I'm gonna do it again!"

"I thought haunted houses were a rip-off," I reminded him.

"Yeah, but this one's cool."

"Lean back," I told him, and he was gone.

"*You* do this for a while," I told Crysti. "I need a break."

"Sure," she said. "Go keep Mom company. She needs all the help she can get."

By now the line of kids looped up and down the driveway and across the grass. Cars were parked along both sides of the street. A steady stream of children and grown-ups poured out the back door.

I wedged my way into the crowded kitchen. Mom was apologizing for the lack of doughnuts, and handing out Oreo cookies instead.

"They're coming from everywhere!" Mom shook her head.

Dad trudged in, his arms loaded with grocery bags. "Come one, come all!" he cried. "Thrills and chills and we pay the bills!"

I couldn't remember the last time I heard Dad joking like this. To my parents, this stampede was a disaster. But it was the sort of calamity that got funnier by the minute.

"I have an announcement to make," Mom said, getting into the spirit. She jumped up on a step stool and towered above the crowd. "This is the *last time* we're doing this! *No haunted house next year!* Spread the word!"

A sigh of disappointment rose from all the kids in the kitchen. "But this is the best one ever!" exclaimed Ryan the Robot. "I'm going through again!"

For the next two hours, Crysti and I took turns by the basement window. A few kids went through twice, or even three times. But Ryan the Robot came back over and over again, so many times I lost count. "You're not collecting a doughnut each time, are you?" I demanded as he readied himself for another slide down the chute.

"Your mom won't give me any more," he said. "I've been through thirty-four times so far. I want to get up to sixty before I quit."

"What for?" The line was building up behind him, but I really wanted to know.

"This is the last year for it," he said. "I've got to pack it all in at once. I'm ten now, and I'll probably live to be seventy. So if I go through the haunted house sixty times, it'll be once for every year of my life that's left."

"Good luck," I said. " 'Bye!" And he whizzed down the slide again.

He was so certain, I marveled, with a wrench of envy. But you could never really count on living to be old. You could wind up in a car accident like Teddy Donovan. Or you could wake up one morning and find out you've got leukemia. . . .

This wasn't only my last year for the haunted house. I could be looking at my last Thanksgiving, my last Christmas, my final birthday. As my friends grew up, went steady, got their driver's licenses, headed off to college — did all of the things that were supposed to happen "someday" — I might not be around anymore. I might miss it all, all the fun and adventure I had assumed would belong to me if I just hung on and waited for "someday" to come.

Suddenly the full weight of it all bore down upon me. I leaned against the wall, overwhelmed, defeated. How could I worry about losing my hair, when I might lose my entire life? For me the future stretched no longer than a swoop down the slide into the basement.

All around me, people laughed and chatted, their lives full of costumes and trick-or-treat. No one else had to worry about bone marrow tests or pills that made them go bald. No one else had to think about the real possibility of dying.

I didn't have to think about it, either, I told myself brusquely. I'd chase leukemia out of my thoughts. Mind over matter, Aunt Cynthia had said. Mind over matter.

"Crysti," I called. "Can you stand here for a while? I want to go through the haunted house myself tonight."

The kitchen was strewn with paper cups and crumpled napkins. The floor was splotched with dirty footprints. Outside, candy wrappers fluttered over the lawn, and the grass was trampled to mud by hundreds of feet.

Aunt Cynthia tossed her witch's hood onto the counter and gulped down a glass of water. "I can't find my normal voice," she squeaked. "Every time I open my mouth a cackle wants to come out!"

"How many people do you think we actually had?" Dad asked. "Don't count Ryan the Robot."

"We went through five dozen doughnuts," Mom said. "Then I started cutting them in half, and they ate four dozen more. Then we ran out, and people *still* kept coming."

"I'll never forget this night!" Crysti was beaming. "I never will, not as long as I live!"

The kitchen seemed strangely empty after almost everyone had left. The four of us kids — our cousins Eric and Carla, Crysti and me — hung around for a while, until the cleanup operation got under control. After I carted out the second bag of trash, Mom told us we could all go and relax.

I was heading out to the den with the others when she called me back. "Jill," she asked, "did you remember your medication after supper?"

I hesitated. "Well, no — I guess not," I said. "I think maybe I forgot."

"Honestly!" Mom exclaimed. "You *know* how important it is! You've got to take some responsibility."

"I know, I know," I said, pulling open the cupboard. As I arranged the containers on the counter, I saw Aunt Cynthia watching me. She was my only ally. "Look at all the junk I've got to take!" I told her. "Four different pills tonight."

Aunt Cynthia studied the containers and shook her head. "You know all this worries me," she said, turning to Mom. "It's chemical overkill. These medications just stifle her body's chance to fight back on its own."

Mom scraped a plate into a fresh garbage bag. Slowly she straightened up. "Cynthia, we know how you feel," she said. "We've discussed all this before."

"Yes," Aunt Cynthia said. "But have you really *thought* about it? Have you really considered your alternatives?"

Mom glanced in appeal to Uncle Howard, who

leaned against the refrigerator with a cup of coffee in his hand. He only shrugged and took another sip. He was better at groaning than talking.

"No," Dad broke in from the doorway. "We haven't considered our alternatives. As far as we're concerned, we're going with the only option there is."

I picked up a dish towel and began wiping the counter. If anyone remembered that I was there, I'd be sent out of the room. And I didn't want to miss a word.

Aunt Cynthia stood up a little taller and put her hands on her hips. "Your minds are closed," she said. "You haven't thought about natural remedies."

"Of course we have!" Mom said. "Exercise — a healthy diet — a good positive attitude — we honestly do believe those things can help, too."

"You have to give them a fair chance," Aunt Cynthia declared. "They can't work against these poisons — "

"Cynthia, please!" Mom begged. "Please don't start this again!"

"It isn't an argument," Aunt Cynthia protested. "I'm not trying to make trouble. I'm trying to *help!*" Their voices were rising higher. I glimpsed a flicker of movement in the dining room, and spied Crysti peering in around Dad's back. Eric and Carla were behind her.

"We're not talking about getting rid of a cold,"

Dad said. "We've got to stick with the program the doctors have laid out. It's the only thing we can do."

Aunt Cynthia refused to back down. "It *isn't* your only choice. If you would just do some reading, talk to some people — "

"Don't you think we've *done* those things!" Mom cried. "Cynthia, you have absolutely no idea what we've been going through!"

"You've let the medical establishment push you into a decision," Aunt Cynthia began. "You've — "

"It's been terrible!" Mom rushed on. Her voice shook with tears. "It's been terribly hard on all of us!"

"I know that. That's why, if you'd just listen — "

"We're doing what we feel is best!" Mom rushed on. "The best thing possible for Jill!"

"It's what you *think* is best!" Aunt Cynthia said. "I'm only trying to tell you there are other ways, other theories — "

"We're not interested in theories," Dad broke in. "We want the facts. And the fact is, medical treatment works better than anything else anybody knows of right now."

"Cynthia," Mom said, "you're my sister — I need your support. If you can't give me that, then you might as well leave this house."

From the TV in the den, a burst of canned

laughter crashed across the sudden stillness. The dish towel had slipped from my hand. I stared at it, a crumpled heap at my feet.

"I'm sorry," Aunt Cynthia said in a low voice. "I think we'd better go."

At last Uncle Howard came to life. He set down his coffee cup and herded Eric and Carla toward the door. Wordlessly Aunt Cynthia gathered up fragments of discarded costumes. No one tried to stop them.

"I'll never figure out your sister!" Dad said, after we said our quick, strained good-byes. "She doesn't know when to quit. She gets a notion into her head — "

"Let's not talk about it," Mom said. "I feel too wrung out. Take your medicine, Jill."

Mom's words echoed in my head: *It's been terribly hard on all of us!* I'd been so bound up in my own misery, I'd hardly thought about what my illness cost the rest of the family. Mom and Dad were doing what they believed was best for me. They believed I should take my pills. All of them, every day. *The best thing possible for Jill . . .*

They were fighting for me. I couldn't let them down.

I went to the sink and filled a glass with water. One by one I counted my pills into my palm. From now on I would take them all, every last one, no matter what happened.

Suddenly the picture of Elizabeth flashed into my mind. For an instant she floated before me, her smile knowing, her head smooth and bald.

One by one I swallowed my prednisone, my antibiotic, and a vitamin capsule. I thought of telling Mom that I hadn't taken my 6-MP this morning. I'd say it was an accident; I just forgot. But this was no time to stir up more trouble.

I wasn't due to take another 6-MP until tomorrow. I'd worry about it in the morning.

I found Crysti in the den, huddled on the couch. She lifted her head. Her face was red and puffy with crying. "I was having so much fun!" she said thinly. "It was — just like old times — and now it's ruined."

"It's not," I insisted. "All the fun parts, they really did happen — "

"It's like when I made you that bouquet last summer," Crysti went on. "I was so happy doing it, and it looked so nice, and then it turned out it was full of ants."

"Mom and Aunt Cynthia have to make up sooner or later," I said. "They're sisters. You know how sisters fight."

Crysti didn't laugh. "Why couldn't we just have one night without anybody feeling sad or being too tired or getting mad. . . . "

"Things always get better if you just wait long enough," I said helplessly.

"Do you ever wish you could run away?" she

asked. "Like just go to some peaceful place where nobody knows you? Then if they didn't pay attention to you it wouldn't matter, because they'd just be strangers anyway."

"What good would it do to run away?" I asked. "You'd just find a lot of new problems out there."

"So what?" Crysti said. "Sometimes I hate living here! I wish I belonged to a different family!"

I thought of Aunt Cynthia, silently gathering her things to go. We'd never had a major family fight like that before, not right in front of everyone. We were crumbling, falling to pieces.

"I guess I don't blame you," I told Crysti. "No matter how bad things are around here, it seems like they always find a way to get even worse."

# 16

The next morning, the backyard looked like Gettysburg after the battle. The trampled grass was strewn with mangled candy wrappers, crumpled napkins, and squashed Styrofoam cups. "I don't suppose we're eligible for government disaster relief," Dad remarked over breakfast. "Looks like we'd better dig in ourselves."

We talked about the cleanup operation — about rakes and rubber gloves, and where were the big bags we used for grass clippings. . . . All the while, I kept thinking of Aunt Cynthia and the pained look on her face when she said good-bye.

Sitting there, pretending that nothing was wrong, I felt currents of tension buzz up and down my spine. The party was definitely over. Nobody joked about the hordes that had pounded through our house last night. And nobody dared to mention Aunt Cynthia's name.

Almost casually I ran a hand through my hair.

A tangled clump came away in my fist. My pillow had been covered with loose strands when I woke that morning. My hair was falling out faster than ever.

Maybe 6-MP wasn't the problem. I'd have to experiment. I'd skip one pill for a while, then another, until I found the culprit. Somehow I'd make sure that I didn't go bald.

From across the table, Crysti was delivering a long, winding story about school. I heard the name Mrs. Nyburg and remembered that was her teacher. Then my thoughts drifted away again. Suppose Dr. Etch figured out what I was doing. My blood work might give me away. I pictured him, frowning from behind his glasses as he handed me the dire truth: *You'll never get better now; you've destroyed your only chance. . . .*

"So can we?" Crysti demanded. "Please?"

For a moment nobody spoke. "Can we what?" Mom asked at last.

"Can we go?" Crysti said. "I just told you." She gazed around the table, from one blank face to another. "About Thanksgiving," she prompted, like a teacher waiting for someone to remember the right answer.

Mom and Dad exchanged a questioning glance. I wasn't the only one who hadn't been listening. Probably they were thinking about hospital bills, or the fight with Aunt Cynthia, or some other worry I couldn't even guess.

Finally Mom said, "Explain it to us again, okay?"

Crysti shoved her chair back from the table. "What's the use?" she cried, springing up. "Nobody pays attention anyway!"

"Crysti, that isn't true," Mom said. "I'm sorry — we were kind of distracted — tell us again."

"Never mind," Crysti said. "We won't be able to go anyway."

"Not if you don't tell us where," Dad pointed out.

"It's in the school bulletin," Crysti said. "You can read about it." She turned and stormed out of the room.

We sat in stunned silence. Crysti's feet thudded up the stairs, and a moment later her door slammed.

"What's going on with her?" Dad asked, shaking his head.

"Give her a few minutes," Mom said. "We can talk when she calms down."

"I'll look for those garbage bags," I said, getting up. "I might as well get started out there."

Mom glanced at my plate. Instantly she focused on my half-eaten slice of toast, and the inquisition began. "Do you feel all right, Jill? Aren't you hungry?"

"I feel fine!" I snapped. "I don't have to eat every scrap of food in front of me, do I?"

"I never said you had to eat every scrap," Mom began. "I only — "

"Haven't we had enough family strife for a while?" Dad asked, scowling.

"Yes," I said and walked defiantly away from my unfinished breakfast.

"Your medication, Jill," Mom reminded me. She didn't even wait to see if I'd forget.

"I know, I know!" I banged open the cupboard and glanced at my chart. Only two pills this morning — 6-MP and prednisone. I'd skip the 6-MP one more time, just to make sure.

Upstairs Crysti's door opened again. She descended slowly, sulkily, and arrived in the kitchen without a word. In one hand she clutched a long yellow sheet of paper.

I took the two containers from the shelf and shook a pill from each into my hand. Crysti waved her paper toward Mom.

"What's that?" Mom asked.

Crysti slapped the paper against her thigh. "You *still* weren't listening!" she cried. "I *said* you have to read the bulletin!"

"Listen, young lady," Dad said sternly. "I don't want to hear that tone of voice around here."

Now was my chance — now, while the three of them were absorbed in each other. I filled my glass at the sink and swallowed the prednisone in one swift gulp.

Then I slipped the 6-MP pill into my pocket.

"We're going to need the rake," I told Dad. "We can scrape everything into one big pile."

I pulled open the back door and stepped onto the porch. "Mom," Crysti said at my back. "Mom, I think Jill didn't take all the pills she's supposed to."

I froze, my hand on the wooden railing. "What?" Mom demanded. "What are you talking about?"

"She didn't," Crysti insisted. "I saw her. She made believe, but she hid one."

My hand dove into my pocket. There was the pill, a tiny, round lump of guilt. I'd destroy the evidence, I thought in a blur of panic. I'd toss it down among the trampled wrappers, where no one would ever find it.

But Dad was on his feet, watching me through the screen door. I couldn't make a move under his relentless gaze. "Jill," he said, and I had never heard him speak with such sternness. "Come here."

I went back inside. When he sounded like that, I had no choice.

"Tell me the truth," he said. "Have you been taking all of your medicine?"

I stared at the pattern of squares and rectangles on the linoleum. I couldn't lie. I couldn't say anything at all.

"Jill, please!" Mom begged. "This is *so* important! You've got to tell us!"

168

With each second that passed, the kitchen grew smaller. There was nowhere to lose myself. I couldn't escape.

"I hate you, Crysti!" I cried, hurling myself toward her. "This is all your fault! Why'd you have to go and open your mouth?"

I seized a thick handful of her hair and yanked hard. Before she could wrench free, I slapped her across the cheek. "Why can't you ever shut up!" I screamed. "Why — "

Dad grabbed my shoulders, but I struggled in his grasp. "You don't even care if my hair falls out!" I shrieked. "You're always the little goody-goody! Running to Mom and Dad if I do the least thing wrong — "

Dad twisted me around to face him. "Jill, stop this," he said, looking me straight in the eye. "I want an answer from you right now. *Have* you been skipping your medication?"

"Yes," I whispered. "Sometimes."

"We'd better call Dr. Echevarria," Mom said, snatching up the phone. "This could be serious!"

"All right," Dad said steadily, "think back. How many pills did you skip?"

"Just the six-MP. I took everything else, honest!"

"How long has this been going on? How many didn't you take?"

"Just yesterday's, and this morning's."

"Yes," Mom was saying into the receiver. "Is

Dr. Echevarria there? . . . Well, I don't know if it's an emergency or not. It might be. . . . Yes . . . "

"Why?" Dad demanded. "Why would you do a thing like that?"

Through the roaring in my ears, it was hard to remember. The room swayed around me, and I might have slid to the floor if Dad hadn't been holding my arms. "My hair's starting to fall out," I muttered. "I can't stand it."

"Your *hair!*" Dad exploded. "Those pills are helping you fight this disease! You're willing to throw away your chance to get well — for the sake of your *hair?*"

"Dr. Echevarria!" Relief flooded Mom's voice. "We've got a bit of a crisis here. . . . No, she seems fine, but we just found out she hasn't been taking all of her six-MP. We've been letting her handle it herself, like you suggested — I mean, we always remind her, she has a tendency to forget, you know — but we don't stand over her and count how many pills she takes. It never occurred to us she wouldn't take them all. We should have watched more closely. . . . Yes, she seems all right. . . . Yes, yes we will. You're sure then it won't cause any — any problems?"

I felt Dad's grip relax. Slowly the room slipped back into focus.

"Thank you," Mom said fervently. "That's very reassuring. . . . All right. . . . Thank you. . . ."

"If it's only one, he says it'll be okay," Mom said. "Thank goodness we found out before it was too late."

What was the matter with me? Had I really been willing to risk my life just to avoid wearing a wig for a couple of months? "I guess I was pretty stupid," I said. "I'll take it from now on. I promise."

"You should be glad you have such a loyal sister," Dad said. "What if she hadn't told us? Suppose you went for weeks without taking your medication, and came out of remission! She may have saved your life!"

He let me go, and I stepped back, bumping against the table. I reached for a chair and held on until I found my balance.

"Now," Dad said, "you'd better take that pill."

I drew it from my pocket. Nestled on my palm it looked like a little round pebble. I bowed my head in humiliation. Slowly I went to the sink, filled a glass, and gulped it down.

Uncertainly I glanced around the room. Mom and Dad were watching. They didn't give me any orders; they simply waited to see what I would do next.

Faintly, like the strains of faraway music, it slipped into my mind. I had to talk to Crysti. I didn't know what I would tell her, but I had to say something.

"Crysti," I called. "Hey, Crys?"

"She must have gone upstairs," Mom said. "I think I saw her go through the dining room."

I went to the bottom of the stairs and shouted up to her. "Crysti! You up there? What are you doing?"

She didn't answer.

"Did she go out?" Dad asked. "I didn't hear the door, did you?"

"No," Mom said. "Not that I was really listening."

"Maybe she's in the basement," I suggested. "She probably started cleaning up." I opened the basement door and hollered down the stairs. "Crysti! Need any help down there?" But my words disappeared in the echoing stairwell.

The attic, I thought with a rush of certainty. That was the place to retreat when things got unbearable. I knew; I'd been there.

I raced up the stairs, pushed my way through the hanging clothes in my closet, and creaked open the attic door. "Crysti!" I cried. But I saw at a glance that the little room under the roof was empty.

Slowly I descended the stairs toward the grown-up voices in the living room. "I'll take a look down the street," Dad was saying. "She's probably at the Shermans'."

Mom opened the front door. She stepped outside and bellowed, "Crysti! *Crystal Jean Marino!*"

I don't know how they had missed the note. It glared up from the dining-room table, a stark white oblong on the tan Formica, commanding our attention. I picked it up, unfolded it, and read:

*Dear Mom, Dad, and Jill,*

*I don't know how to explain anything. It just seems like everything I do makes things worse here. So I think I better go away for a while. Don't worry about me. I'll be all right.*

*Love*
*Crysti*

"Mom!" I cried. "Dad! Come here quick! Crysti ran away!"

# 17

"**S**he couldn't have gotten far," Dad kept saying, but Crysti wasn't in any of the obvious places. She wasn't at the Shermans'; she wasn't hanging around in any of the stores downtown; she wasn't moping on the grass in the square, waiting to be found. Dad called the college and canceled his eleven-o'clock class: "A family emergency," he explained, and a prickle of fear crawled down my back.

We stood in a huddle in the kitchen, too shaken to think clearly. This couldn't be happening, I thought dizzily. I'd been mean to Crysti this morning, I admitted it. But had I done anything terrible enough to drive her away from home? We used to fight all the time before I got sick. But she never before left a note on the table and ran away.

Mom spread out her hands, empty and helpless, and picked up the phone. "We'd better call the police."

Dad shook his head. "Let's not panic," he said.

"She isn't a baby. She's probably hiding out in somebody's backyard, and when she's good and ready she'll come home."

"You read the papers!" Mom exclaimed. "You know the things that can happen! There are crazy people out there . . . "

"Well," Dad said, glancing up at the clock, "give it another fifteen minutes."

"I'll walk around the block," I offered. "Maybe I'll see her wandering around somewhere."

Last night the street swarmed with children in Halloween finery. But now it was wrapped in the stillness of a sleepy Saturday morning. When a car whispered past, it only made me feel more alone.

I walked slowly, peering into yards with swing sets and barking dogs and white picket fences. A wind whipped my face, and bare autumn branches gestured overhead. Today was the first of November. Last summer seemed endlessly far away, like a magical kingdom from a story I had nearly forgotten.

Nothing had ever been right since that first visit to see Dr. Lewis. Our house was a mire of worry, scolding, and disappointment. I either felt sick or lived with the dread that I would suddenly feel sick again. Mom and Dad were tense, frightened, tired, and sad all at once. No one had the energy for extra, impractical things. We had tried to have fun last night, but it had ended in disaster.

If I were Crysti, I'd run away, too. I'd put a thousand miles between myself and the demon that haunted our house. But I couldn't run. The demon was always with me, wherever I went.

Crysti wouldn't go far, I assured myself. She'd get cold and hungry, and she'd come home. When I opened the back door she'd be sitting at the kitchen table, looking sheepish and a little scared. Dad and Mom would lecture her, and she'd be grounded for a month. But they'd be too relieved to be really angry.

When I walked back into the warmth of the kitchen, I gazed around in disbelief. Dad was talking on the phone, and Mom stood anxiously beside him.

"Crystal Jean Marino," Dad was saying. "She's ten. She's — oh, she's — " He turned to Mom. "They want her height and weight."

"Four-ten," Mom said. "She weighs sixty-eight pounds."

"Four-ten, sixty-eight," Dad repeated mechanically. "She had on — " He turned to Mom again. "What on earth does she have on today?"

"She took her green nylon jacket," Mom said. "And she had on tennis shoes and blue jeans. And her hair's in a ponytail."

"She had one of those barrettes with a pink ribbon," I added.

"No, she's never done anything like this before. . . . Well, of course I'm sure! I live with the kid, don't I? If she were a habitual runaway, don't you think I'd notice?" Dad was practically shouting now.

"Read them her note," Mom said.

But Dad was saying, "Yes, please. We'll be here. Yes."

"They're sending somebody over," he said when he hung up. "They want to ask us some questions."

"She wasn't outside," I said pointlessly. "I looked everywhere I could think of."

They barely glanced my way. "What was the name of that little girl she used to play with last year?" Dad mused. "She had real light-brown hair, almost blonde. Molly, or Dolly, or Polly . . ."

"They lived over on Pleasant Street," Mom said eagerly. "Molly Sanders! I'll give them a call!"

Molly Sanders hadn't seen Crysti since the haunted house last night, but her mother gave Mom a list of names and numbers to call. There was nothing for me to do but listen to the same tired question over and over, knowing time after time what the answer would be.

Our house had seen so much turmoil lately — we should all be accustomed to it by now. But today, for the first time, I was merely part of the background. The turmoil swept past me, as if I were alone on an island. Crysti's name wove through every conversation. Crysti was in everyone's thoughts.

With a stab of recognition, I knew how Crysti must have felt through the long, tortured crisis of my illness. Not forgotten exactly, not unloved, but simply eased aside to make room for more pressing matters. Not quite unimportant, but not a priority, either. Expected to behave, to cooperate, to help the day pass smoothly. To wait her turn.

Most of the time, my little sister had done those things. She'd complained now and then, like the time we didn't go to Cedar Point. But for the most part she slipped into the shadows. I'd been so caught up with my own problems that I'd scarcely given her a thought. Looking back, I couldn't recall Mom or Dad spending much time with her, either. They hadn't gone to her Columbus Day skit. And whatever that Thanksgiving program was that she'd been talking about this morning — they hadn't even listened to her. They'd always been there for me, though, whenever I needed them.

For that matter, they were there for me a lot of times when I didn't need them at all. They fussed constantly. They were always telling me to be careful, checking me for bruises, reminding me to take my pills. I might be sick, but I *was* thirteen years old. I could handle responsibility.

Well, I hadn't handled it very well so far. When it was time for a trip to the hospital, I hid in the attic. They let me take my pills by myself, and I tried to trick them.

I sank onto my bed. Fighting and grumbling, complaining every step of the way, I had made the situation as bad as possible for the whole family.

Leukemia wasn't the only demon that plagued our household. There was another monster, selfish and mean and endlessly demanding. It was a creature of my own creation, and I had let it make the rules.

Downstairs the doorbell rang. A murmur of voices reached me — Mom and Dad talking to a stranger who introduced himself as Sergeant Lambert. I crept into the hall and listened from the top of the stairs.

"Well, Officer, I guess she *has* been kind of upset lately," Dad was saying. "Our other daughter — Jill — she's been sick . . . " His voice fell, but I knew what came next — the brief, painful explanation, the policeman's awkward sympathy.

"May I talk to her?" Sergeant Lambert asked after a moment. "To Jill? Can she — "

"Oh, sure," Dad said. "She's okay." I was already on my way down when he called, "Jill?"

The officer sat at the kitchen table, scratching notes on a clipboard. Age . . . height . . . weight . . . friends . . . hobbies . . .

At last he leveled his gaze at me and asked,

"Did Crysti ever say anything to you? Did she tell you she was unhappy, that she was planning to do this?"

"Last night," I said, remembering aloud. "She said she wished she could run away."

"Did she say where she wanted to go?"

I shook my head. "No," I said. "I guess I'm the last person she'd tell."

"Well," Officer Lambert persisted, "where do you think she'd go? Does she have any friends your folks don't know about?"

"Try to think," Mom prodded.

My mind was blank, useless. "I don't know of any," I said,

"All right then," said Officer Lambert, pushing back his chair. "We'll make some calls and see what we come up with. Make sure there's somebody here at all times. We'll check back in an hour or so."

"You don't have any ideas . . . " Mom began. Her voice faded.

"Can't give you any answers yet, if that's what you mean," the officer said, shaking his head. "But this sort of thing happens a lot. You never know — she might walk in the back door as I go out the front."

We trailed him out to the porch and waved as he climbed into the squad car. Inside again, I half expected to hear the back door bang open and Crysti's feet thump across the kitchen floor. But the house was quiet. It gave no clues.

The afternoon was an agony of waiting. Each time the phone rang, Dad pounced on the receiver with a brusque, "Yes?" Once it was one of Mom's real-estate clients; once it was someone trying to sell aluminum siding; and one time it was an old woman who wanted to speak with Madeline. At one-forty-five Sergeant Lambert called to ask if we had any news yet. It was his way of telling us he had nothing to report.

Aunt Cynthia arrived at three o'clock, and she and Mom gave each other a big, tearful hug in the front vestibule. Mom ushered her out to the kitchen, and she sat with us, sipping coffee, not talking much. There wasn't much left to say. All we could do was wait.

I thought I knew about being afraid. I'd known real terror each time they admitted me to Memorial Hospital. I shuddered when I thought about spinal taps and bone marrow tests, and trembled with dread when I waited for some heartless lab report that held my fate. But that afternoon I discovered a different kind of fear — the fear of losing someone else. I had never paid much attention to Crysti when she was around. But if she disappeared, if we never found her again, she would leave a terrible hole in our lives that could never be filled.

If only Crysti would come back, I thought, I'd make up for all the times I was ever mean. I'd never ignore her again. I'd be sure to find time to listen!

I glanced at the clock. The hands had shifted, almost imperceptibly, and I realized that it was time for my next pill. I went to the cupboard, got out the container, and swallowed it without a word. When I glanced up, Mom was watching me with a tired smile. "I remembered," I said. "It's easy, really. Nothing to it."

Aunt Cynthia turned to Mom. "I've been thinking," she said cautiously. "About this treatment Jill's on."

"What about it?" Mom asked. She sounded cautious, too.

"I got to thinking," Aunt Cynthia floundered. "I just don't trust doctors very much. I always feel better if I can be in charge when anything's wrong."

She stopped, and I braced myself for another explosion. But Mom didn't argue with her. She just shrugged and began rinsing some dishes.

"But the trouble is," Aunt Cynthia went on, "if somebody's really sick, where else do you go? I guess if it were one of my kids, I'd do exactly what you're doing."

"I know that a lot of what you've been saying is right," Mom said. "But we have to stick this out. It's the only thing that makes sense."

And then the doorbell rang.

They stood on the front porch. Sergeant Lambert looked bigger than I remembered. When he stepped inside, he overflowed the vestibule with his glad, booming voice and his enormous grin. Shrinking behind him, her face flushed, her hair disheveled, and one tennis shoe untied, was my only sister, Crysti.

# 18

Crysti huddled on a kitchen chair, looking sheepish and scared, as we all fluttered around her. Mom and Dad shouted and hugged her and scolded some more. We all pelted her with questions, but at first her short, muffled answers didn't tell us much. "She was at the county children's shelter," Sergeant Lambert explained. "She called from a pay phone somewhere and one of the social workers went out and got her."

"The county home!" Mom exclaimed in horror. "Oh, *Crysti!* How *could* you?" She looked as if she was going to cry.

Aunt Cynthia touched her arm. "She's *safe,* that's the main thing," she said quietly. "Nobody's blaming you. It'll get sorted out."

"Now *that,*" Mom said, caught somewhere between tears and laughter, "is what I mean by *support!*"

Later that evening, after everyone had gone, Mom made pancakes for supper. As the kitchen filled with the warm, homey smell, Crysti told her story. She had seen a TV announcement about the children's shelter and copied down the phone number. She had kept it for weeks, convinced that she might want to use it someday. Today the time had come.

I had a pretty good idea what her reasons were. Somehow I didn't want to hear her list them out loud. "What was it like there?" I asked. "I kind of picture one big room with little cubicles full of bunk beds."

"I never got to see the dormitory part," Crysti said. "First I was in the social worker's office. She kept asking me questions, but I didn't want to tell her my name or anything. So then she let me go out in the TV room. It was real noisy. I was sitting there, and all of a sudden these two girls got into a fight. I don't know what it was about. They just started screaming at each other and punching and scratching — it was awful. And then this other girl, her name was Beth, she says to me, 'Don't mind them. They do that all the time — they're sisters.' And I thought, hey, at least I get along with my sister better than *that!*"

I laughed uneasily and tried to think of a snappy comeback. There was none.

"The more I talked to Beth, the more I got the idea I didn't belong there," Crysti said. "I mean, things here started to look better and better, you know? Then the social worker sent for me again, and said she'd called the police and that they were looking for somebody who sounded a lot like me. I guess I started crying," she added, embarrassed. "I thought, what a stupid thing to do, make all this trouble for everybody. . . ."

"So you told them," I said, trying to make it easier for her. "You said you're Crystal Jean Marino, four-ten, sixty-eight pounds, wearing blue jeans, and tennis shoes."

"They had it all down," she said in awe. "Even my ponytail. My pink ribbon's gone," she added as I noticed for the first time that her hair hung loose. "I gave it to Beth for a good-bye present. She was my friend the whole time."

The "sorting out," as Aunt Cynthia called it, wasn't easy. That first night Mom and Dad spent an hour talking to Crysti alone. I never knew what they said, but she finally came upstairs, sniffling, and shut her door. She probably needed to be alone, I told myself, picking up a book. But after two pages I knew I was making excuses. I crossed the hall and tapped at her door.

"It's me," I said. "Okay if I come in?"

"If you want."

She sat in a chair by the window, a blanket over her knees. Her cheeks had a pale, hollow look, and her eyes were red. Anybody seeing her for the first time might have thought *she* was the sister who was sick.

"Hi," I said awkwardly. "Did you catch it downstairs?"

"It wasn't too bad," she said. "I thought I'd be grounded for the rest of my life. But mostly they just kept saying I ought to talk to them if I'm upset instead of just running away — all that kind of stuff."

"I think Mom felt like it was all her fault," I said. I hesitated. "You know she wouldn't want to blame me."

"Well, *you* can't help — " Crysti began.

"I can do a *little* better, I bet," I said and tried to laugh. "I can't blame it all on prednisone. I guess I kind of quit trying to be — you know — a regular person."

For the first time Crysti smiled, a real, honest grin. It was as if my admission had opened a door, and the old Crysti came bounding out at last. "It was kind of exciting, running away," she said. "I actually *did* it, you know what I mean? I thought about it and thought about it and then I did it! I kept looking around the place and thinking, I can't believe I'm really *here!* . . . I won't ever do it again — but it sure was an adventure!"

When I woke up the next morning, I felt something tickling my chin. In the pale sunlight that crept through my curtains I saw that my pillow was covered with great clumps of hair.

My heart thumping, I ran to the mirror. My head looked ragged, and when I touched it, hair came out in my fingers.

I rushed downstairs and found Mom on the phone, making last-minute arrangements for an open house that afternoon. She took one look at me and gasped. "I'll call you back," she said. "I've got to go."

"This is horrible!" I moaned. "Why should I lose my hair *now?* It was fine in the hospital, and the drugs there were stronger!"

"Dr. Echevarria warned us this could happen," Mom said, but she called him anyway. No, he couldn't reduce my 6-MP. It wouldn't save my hair, anyway. The hair loss, he explained, was probably a lingering effect of the vincristine I had in the hospital. I would lose all of my hair, now that the process had begun. But, he assured us, it *would* grow back.

"How can I go to school?" I wailed. "How can I face anybody?"

"You can get a hairpiece," Crysti suggested. "You could even pick out a new color."

"Yeah, right," I grumbled. "Have they got them in green for us Martians?" But even as I spoke, I knew that going bald wasn't the worst thing that could happen.

I went back to school on Monday, wearing a dark-brown wig. It felt strange and itchy on my naked skull, and I couldn't help reaching up from time to time to make sure it hadn't slipped out of place. I promised myself I'd never step outside on a windy day.

"You look *gorgeous!*" gushed Iris Block. "Like somebody in a fashion magazine! You can hardly even tell that's not your real hair!" I wished very hard that I could believe her.

Through the days that followed, I found myself thinking more and more about Elizabeth. She always seemed so confident, coasting through the halls in her wheelchair, challenging people with her bold, bald stare. When it came to leukemia, Elizabeth was a pro. I wondered when I would see her again. Like me, she was always in and out of the hospital for tests and treatments. In my mind I stored up a pile of questions to ask the next time we were together.

The night before Thanksgiving, we all went with Crysti's class to a special holiday concert by a children's choir from Russia. I expected to be bored, but Crysti really wanted us all to go, so I didn't argue about it. According to the program, the kids were on tour in the United States for three months, and this was one of their first stops. They looked utterly happy, beaming out at us from the stage. They sang songs in Russian and French, and for their grand finale they presented a medley of pieces in English. Their voices seemed to fill the auditorium with pure joy.

"This was great!" I told Crysti on our way back to the parking lot. "I'm so glad you got us to come."

Crysti grinned. She looked as happy as one of those choir kids from Russia herself.

A few days later, I woke with a sore throat and a dry, hacking cough. "It's just the flu or something," I insisted when Mom came at me with a thermometer. But as soon as she took my temperature, she headed for the phone. By noon I found myself tucked into bed on Pediatric Oncology — needles, IV tubes, and all.

"You're perfectly right, love," said Barbara when she came in to check me over. "You have the flu. But when you're on anticancer drugs, we don't take any chances. Can't let the germs get a toehold, you know."

It was discouraging to be back in the hospital, so swiftly and unexpectedly. Apart from losing my hair and gaining a few nasty canker sores from my weekly methotrexate pills, I'd been feeling almost normal. Still, if I *had* to be in a hospital, Memorial wasn't really so bad. It was nice to see Barbara again, to hear her say, "Buck up, love," in that rich British accent of hers. And when Big Mac barreled in, exclaiming, "So you like us so much you can't stay away!" I could almost have hugged her. Mom and Dad didn't need to stay overnight with me this time. In fact, they just dropped in and out during regular visiting hours, and I didn't feel frightened. By now I knew I was among friends.

They gave me intravenous antibiotics ("the best weapons we've got against bugs," as Dr. Echevarria put it), and by Thursday my temperature was normal. "Your remission is still holding," Dr. Etch explained as he scribbled in the chart at the foot of my bed. "But I want to keep you here another day or two. Just to be on the safe side."

"Have they still got that group in the afternoons?" I heard myself asking him. "You know — the one you told me about?"

"The support group? Sure. Three o'clock tomorrow down in the lounge. Why don't you drop in?"

"I'm thinking about it," I said. "Maybe I will."

At three o'clock the next afternoon, I sauntered down the hall, feeling marvelously light and free now that my IV was finally disconnected. I thought I would just peek into the lounge and see who was there, but Mrs. Branford was on the lookout. "Jill!" she exclaimed. "I'm glad to see you! Come on in!" There was no way to refuse.

Eagerly I searched the room for Elizabeth. Four curious faces studied me as I took a seat, but hers was not among them. I did recognize Jessica, the girl I'd met there last summer. Her friend Vince sat beside her. To my relief I saw that he now sported a full head of hair. I remembered how bald he'd been in August and knew there was hope for me.

I wasn't the only newcomer. Beside me, a girl of about twelve sat hunched in a wheelchair, staring at the floor. Mrs. Branford introduced her as Tamra and explained that this was her first time in the hospital. Tamra barely glanced up when we all murmured, "Hi."

"We had the craziest Thanksgiving at our house!" Jessica announced. "We had eighteen people over, and my dad went to take out the turkey, and it was raw! The oven'd gone out! We ended up with sweet potatoes and cranberry sauce and hamburgers!"

"We went to my grandparents'," said Justin, a skinny boy in faded jeans. "Everybody came, even my cousins from California." He paused and added, "I guess they thought it might be their last chance to see me or something."

"Don't you just hate that!" Jessica cried, thumping the arm of her chair. "I mean, why do people have to *dwell* on it all the time? If I come in here for a spinal tap, I've got relatives pouring in from Maine and Kansas and Florida — "

"They quit Florida and come up to Cleveland?" Vince demanded. "Man, they really must love you!"

A ripple of laughter swept around our little circle. A smile even flickered across Tamra's brooding face.

"Hey, Vince, what'd you do with your T-shirt?" Justin asked suddenly. "I figure I might be needing it pretty soon."

Jessica turned to me and explained, "Vince had this shirt made up that says: BALD IS BEAUTIFUL."

"You're kidding!" I cried, and my hand flew to my wig. "That's weird!"

"Listen, what have you got against baldness?" Vince asked. "Some of my best friends are among the hairless!" This time everybody laughed. Even me.

"Speaking of medicine," Vince said when we were quiet again. "I've got an announcement to make." As all eyes turned to him, he got to his feet. "Hear ye, hear ye! I'm graduating next week!"

As the others broke into a joyous cheer, Tamra and I stared at him blankly. "What he means," Mrs. Branford explained, "is that he's all finished with treatment."

"You mean you're cured?" I demanded. "You're all better, forever?"

"They never say the word *cure*," Vince said ruefully. "I'm in 'stable long-term remission.' Anyway, it means I'm through with this place for good!"

"You're one of the six," Jessica murmured. "The six of ten in the statistics."

Her words fell eerily into the sudden silence. I glanced around our little circle, counting. There were five of us here today. Each one of us faced the same set of odds. Perhaps all five of us would be lucky, would find our way to "stable long-term remission" someday. Six out of ten . . .

"Is taking the medication really bad?" Tamra said suddenly in a small, scared voice.

Her eyes darted around the circle, searching our faces for the truth. She looked absolutely terrified. I longed to put my arms around her and tell her that everything was going to be all right. But I couldn't make any promises.

"It's pretty yucky," I admitted. "But you get through it. And it really helps you get better."

For a little while we passed medication stories back and forth. Jessica and Justin said there was nothing worse than asparaginase, and Vince said we hadn't seen anything till we got adramycin. It was the first time I'd ever talked to other people who lived with those medications day by day. They spoke their names as if they were annoying acquaintances who had to be tolerated, though they dropped in too often and stayed too long.

Finally, when there was a lull in the talk, Mrs. Branford said, "I'm afraid I have some sad news to share with you."

Instantly tension crackled through the room. I

bent forward, my hands tight on my lap. I didn't belong here, I reminded myself. I only stopped in to see what was going on. . . . Whatever it was, their sad news had nothing to do with me. . . .

"It's Elizabeth, isn't it?" Jessica said in a flat, heavy voice.

Mrs. Branford nodded slowly. "We got a call this morning," she said. "Elizabeth died last night. At home."

*Elizabeth . . . died . . . Elizabeth . . .*

"Did she have a lot of pain?" Vince asked.

"Her mother told me her last few days were very peaceful," Mrs. Branford said. "Two weeks ago she had her seventeenth birthday party, with all her friends from school, and it was a very happy time for her."

"I went to her flute recital in September," Jessica said. "She was so good! Everybody said so! Her teacher gave her a big bouquet."

"She was my roommate the first time I came in here." I hadn't meant to speak; I hadn't known I could manage to say my thoughts out loud. "I didn't like her at first. She was so — so — " I hunted for the right word, "so *certain*. As if nothing ever bothered her really, or scared her, or got her down. It made me mad in a way. Like everybody expected me to be just as brave and fearless as she was."

"She wasn't fearless," Jessica assured me. "She said once that when they told her she had leukemia

195

she wanted to jump out the window, only she was on the first floor."

"I've been thinking about her so much this past week," I said. "I wanted to see her today!" I could no longer hold back the tears. They slid down my cheeks and I didn't try to stop them.

"Elizabeth was somebody special," Jessica said.

So was Jessica, I realized — so were Vince, and Justin, and Tamra. We were all special, every one of us — and we were all in danger. Elizabeth had lost her last battle. The rest of us were still fighting.

"It's not just Elizabeth making me cry," I told them. "I think I'm crying for all of us! None of us asked for this! None of us did anything to deserve it! But here we are, and nobody really knows what's going to happen to any of us!"

"You can say that again," Vince said. "Nobody knows. Nobody knows."

*Elizabeth*, I thought, and her name filled my mind, swelled as big as the whole world.

# 19

Maybe there are moments in life better than leaving the hospital, but I don't think I've known one yet. I love arguing with the nurses about the ridiculous rule that says you have to go to the front door in a wheelchair, no matter how well and strong you feel. I love my tingling impatience as the orderly pushes me across the lobby, my feet hungry to touch the ground, to carry me out and away. And then there is the first breath of real fresh air. The weather doesn't matter; sunshine or sleet, it's all glorious when you've lived for days or weeks on the stale air in a room sealed up against the world outside. When I stand up at last, drenched in the noise of the city street, I know that I am really alive and on my way again.

This time I went home on a Saturday morning, the day after my first group meeting. Dad picked me up, and on the way back to Oberlin we stopped at one of those thirty-one flavors ice-cream places.

I had two scoops of Swiss chocolate almond, and felt I couldn't be any happier.

Crysti came running to greet me when I stepped in the back door. "How was it this time?" she asked as we went inside. "Was it as bad as before?"

"Well — " I hesitated. "I don't exactly *like* the place, but — actually everybody was really nice. It could have been a lot worse."

"I made up a new song," she announced, pouring herself a glass of milk. "You want to hear it?"

"Yeah, sure." I was still trying to keep the resolution I made the day Crysti ran away from home. And really, it wasn't so hard to listen to her now and then. Every once in a while she had something interesting to say.

"Am I allowed to hear this, or should I leave the room?" Dad asked. I had a feeling he and Mom had each made the same resolution.

Crysti tugged at her ponytail. "Well, I guess you can stay," she said at last. "All right, here goes." She stood up very straight, her back to the kitchen sink, and sang in her high, clear voice:

*When the back door opens,*
*When the doorbell rings,*
*When we're finally all together,*
*Then the whole house sings.*

*When everybody's talking,*
*When each one wears a smile,*
*Then I know that we're together,*
*Home and happy for a while.*

*When I see . . . When I see . . .*

Crysti trailed off into nervous giggles. "I forgot the last verse!" she said, covering her face with her hands.

"Hey," I said, "that's really a nice song. I mean it." And it was. Coming at me like that, in my first giddy hours out of the hospital, it made my eyes sting with tears.

"You really like it? You're not just saying that?" she asked, studying my face.

"Since when have I been known to say things just to be nice?" I demanded and gave her a hug that startled us both.

After I unpacked my hospital bag, I headed over to Amanda's house. Mr. Marlewski stepped out on his back porch just as I was clambering over the fence. "I'm going to start charging you girls a toll," he called, but he was grinning. He didn't ask me how I was doing, or try to stretch out the conversation because he felt sorry for me. He acted the way he used to, in the days before I got leukemia.

Amanda and I went straight up to her room,

and she popped a cassette into the machine. Somehow music always made it easier to talk.

"What did I miss all week?" I asked, sprawling on the rug. "What's the latest at school?"

Amanda leaped straight into a story. "We had the weirdest substitute for math!" she exclaimed. "She was really hyper! Like she's bouncing all over the room, looking at everybody's work, talking nonstop, back and forth, up and down. . . . So John Tilman shoots a paper airplane across the room, and it gets her right between the eyes! She had a total fit!"

"Did she know it was him?"

"No, that's just it. She starts marching up and down the rows, and she stands over each kid one by one and she goes, 'Was it you? . . . Was it you? . . . Was it you?' So naturally everybody says no — especially John — and finally she goes, 'I'm going to find out who did it, if I have to bring in a detective!' "

I could just picture John Tilman, bending innocently over his math book. I wished I'd been there to see it all. I missed a lot of fun, being out of school so much.

"So did she?" I asked. "Did she call in the FBI or what?"

"Tune in Monday," Amanda said. "Hey, are you coming back right away?"

"Sure. Why not?"

"I should know not to believe Iris Block,"

Amanda said. "I let her get me all worried."

I pushed myself into a sitting position. "Why? What's she saying now?"

"Oh — " Amanda looked embarrassed. "She was going around telling everybody you're getting worse. She said you might not come back to school again, and she was going to organize a club of kids to visit you, so you'd have company every day."

"I guess she means well," I sighed. "I mean, it's nice of her to be concerned and all, but she's so — so — "

"She's so Iris!" Amanda exclaimed, and we both laughed.

"Well, I'll have to disappoint her," I said. "The doctor says I'm fine. I can go back to school, swimming, everything."

"Fine?" Amanda repeated uncertainly. Then, with rising excitement, she asked, "You mean you're all over it finally?"

"I'm all over the flu," I said. "My counts are good, I'm still in remission. But I'm still on chemo, too. I don't graduate from treatment for — oh, years! Two years, three years, they won't even guess yet."

"Oh." Amanda picked up a stuffed lion, turned it in her hands, and set it on her pillow again. "I thought for a second, I thought maybe you meant you were *better*. That the whole thing was all done."

"No," I said. "I still have leukemia."

"I wish you didn't," Amanda said simply.

"Me, too," I said.

Day by day, December unfurled toward Christmas. Reindeer pranced in the store windows on Main Street, and Crysti spent a lot of time poring over magazines and making wish lists. It was easy to think of things to give her — she loved scary books and Barbies and china horses for the collection on her bookcase. But Mom and Dad were impossible. Mom said she'd like a new scarf or a pair of gloves. Dad was even more uninspired; every year he asked for socks and Old Spice shaving lotion. I wandered around the square, peering into display windows, waiting to spot the perfect gift.

Not that I was any better than Mom or Dad when it came to ideas. In other years I'd been as excited as Crysti, imagining wonderful surprises beneath the tree. But now the pretty dresses and sweaters and knickknacks in the store windows failed to dazzle me. They were only objects, after all — lifeless things. Somehow I didn't long for presents anymore. Maybe it was part of turning into a grown-up.

A week before Christmas, all of us on the swim team went out for pizza. It was one of those good, rich times, all of us jammed into a booth, reminiscing about the past year and planning the season ahead. We'd beat Elyria without any problem.

But Painesville was going to be tough. "Painesville's a pain," said Katie Rosario, and for some reason it was very funny, and Cindy got giggling so much she almost choked on her Sprite.

Cautiously I glanced at Larry, sitting across the table from me. He hardly looked in my direction. He never really *had* noticed me, even before I got sick. Back then I was just one of the kids on the team, almost beneath his notice. I hadn't lost his regard when I passed out in the middle of that race last summer; he'd never thought much of me in the first place. And suddenly, as I watched him shoveling in his fourth slice of pepperoni, I knew that I didn't care. I hadn't cared about Larry for a long time now.

"I have something to announce," Sue, the other assistant coach, said, setting down her glass. "I got a letter today — and I've been accepted at Michigan!"

"You mean the University of?" I asked.

"Right. Ann Arbor." Sue's cheeks glowed with excitement.

"You'll get to live away from home," Cindy said with envy. "Nobody telling you to clean your room, get enough sleep, eat everything on your plate . . . "

"Watch out, world!" Larry said. "Here she comes!"

Sue blushed. It wasn't only excitement. I guess she felt a little awkward, being the center of attention. But she couldn't keep quiet. "It's a huge campus," she said. "I don't know how I'll ever get used to it. But my cousin's up there, so I'll know somebody. She's already telling me which dorm to request. And they've got all the courses I want — a terrific drama department, and a great athletics program. . . . "

Her words danced around me like snowflakes. Sue spoke with such confidence about the future. She claimed years by the handful, stacking them up, filling them with hopes and plans. For her, Michigan was only the beginning of a story that had no end.

I didn't care about Christmas presents. I didn't even crave an admiring glance from Larry. I wanted only to talk about the future the way Sue was talking now. Drivers' ed . . . college . . . summer jobs . . . my first apartment on my own . . . I wanted to know that all those things waited for me out there, that someday they would be within reach.

For a moment I let myself play with the thought — a Christmas promise, wrapped up in shiny paper with a ribbon and a card. *To: Jill Marino / From: The Powers Above / One life, threescore and ten.*

There were no promises. Dr. Echevarria said so at the start, the day after my first bone marrow test. There were no guarantees, but there was hope. I could build my future on that.

I thought back over the long months since last summer, months I had spent raging at my own weakness, at the fate that had handed leukemia to me. Now my anger was dimming, slipping quietly out of the way to make room for this new resolve that swept all through me. As Sue chattered on, I knew I would do everything in my power to get well. Bone marrow tests and spinal taps and IV medications and even my wig were a fair price to pay, if they would buy me a future.

Elizabeth had paid the price, I reminded myself. She paid and paid, and now she was gone.

But while she was alive, she lived. She lived every minute.

"They want us to get out of here," Katie observed. "Look, there are people lining up for tables."

I took a last bite of my pizza. It was cold and rubbery, and the crust had turned to cardboard. It was time to go.

Slowly, noisily, we trooped to the door. "Wow! It's windy!" Katie exclaimed. "It's enough to knock you down!"

In the next instant, my scalp tingled with cold, and I saw my wig scurrying up the sidewalk like a big dark-brown cat. "Help!" I shrieked, clapping my hands over my bald head. "Catch it, somebody!"

Sue and Katie both started running, the rest of us pounding after them down the pavement. One of my worst nightmares had come true. But as the wig bounded and zigzagged with a will of its own, I began to laugh.

"Quick!" I shouted. "Quick, before it gets away!"

"Gotcha!" Katie cried with a pounce. She held the wig high and gave it a vigorous shake. "I hope that'll teach it a lesson!"

"Thanks," I said as she handed it back to me. "You saved the day."

I ran my fingers through the tangled hair, brushing loose a couple of pebbles. Then I planted the wig firmly in place and held it down with one hand, not to take any chances.

"All set?" Sue asked. "I'll give you a ride."

"All set," I told her. "Watch out, world! Here I come!"